MW01172406

An Angel for Aliens

By

Robert Gallagher

An Angel for Aliens

Table of Content

An Angel for Aliens

Acknowledgement

Chris Purcell. Editor & Proofreader

Chapter 1 – "Ten reasons you don't want to meet an alien."

I was stunned to find out the some of the first official UFO studies were in Latin. Thanks to years in a Catholic grade school, I recognized it as Latin, but I was ever so grateful to find out that there were completed translations for most of the more significant works. I guess it makes sense to me now that I know how long such phenomena have been observed and who was keeping track, but I'm getting ahead of myself. Let's start with introductions.

My name is Lee Andrews. I was teaching physics at a medium size Catholic university in the Midwest. I'm not going to name it because honestly the job wasn't that great. I mean it could have been a nice place to work; it was a good school. I was doing some teaching, some research, writing a few articles that might help me get tenure – and make a few extra bucks.

No, it wasn't the school that was my problem. Money was really my issue – and I own it as my problem, the school wasn't particularly stingy – but I was broke, worse than broke. It wasn't because I spent all my money on a wild lifestyle filled with vice and depravity or even just the occasional night on the town. No, I was just actually pretty dull.

I had gotten through grad school on scholarships and part time jobs. I was proud of myself that I hadn't racked up a mountain of student loan debt. OK, maybe it was a small hill of debt, but I got my current job right after I finished my Ph D, and at that time I could see hints of greener grass on the other side of that hill. Then my mom got sick.

It was just the two of us by then – me and mom. Dad had passed away during my senior year in high school. My older brother had already left home to join the military. We rarely ever heard from him and after Dad's funeral, he never came home again. Though the details are still a bit hazy for me, about two years later he was reported missing and about a year after that we were told that he was presumed dead. We never had much of an extended family and now that I think about it, our family members seem to have an eerie tendency to die relatively young. Maybe I should have considered that more carefully before I changed jobs, but again I'm getting ahead of myself.

To put it mildly, whatever insurance we had sucked. Over the two years when mom got so terribly sick, the medical bills and nursing home care cost a not small fortune. She was my mom, all I had, and I wanted the best for her. I don't regret any of my choices and the care she was given. The obscenely high price for all of that is a burden I chose to bear. The articles I write, and some side tutoring, brought in a little extra cash and that helped, but I still expected to be living on ramen noodles the rest of my life.

The articles I write for the more scholarly publications are under my own name, Dr. Lee Andrews PhD, but – and I hate to use the term – for the "dumbed down" ones that I write for more popular consumption, I go by "Andy Leland." Yeah, that's me [*sigh*], the guy who writes about whether *"aliens are messing with our climate"* or *"10 reasons you really don't want to meet an alien."* They aren't poorly written or even inaccurate but I'm pretty sure that my academic colleagues would find them "unbecoming a real scholar." In fact, that is exactly what the dean of the science department told me in private when I accidentally confessed to him at a faculty cocktail party that I was doing some articles under a pen name. That's not something I normally tell people. I'm not even sure how that came up in a conversation, but I'm not much of a drinker and I might have over indulged that night. And, of course, I managed to bare my soul to the head of my department. Thank God that he was the only one to whom I let that slip; he was a good guy and I counted on him not to gossip about my alter ego.

Dean Peltz also knew about my mom and my subsequent financial situation. He said he was proud of me for being such a loving son and he wished the university could pay me more money to help out because he would like to keep me on the staff there. Looking back now, I not sure if that comment was supposed to be consoling or a warning. At that point, I hadn't planned on changing jobs, so I found his words comforting. I liked teaching and being around people – because otherwise I was very much alone in the world.

I had received a few offers for some research positions that paid a lot more than the university. I briefly considered them [*especially when feasting on those ramen noodles*] but I didn't relish the idea of selling myself to some greedy corporation where I would spend all my time in a lab researching gadgets or toys to con the consumers out of their hard-earned money. [*Yeah, you're right, that sounded harsh. I know that researchers like that can make discoveries that really improve life for a lot of people. But, you see, mom was quite the liberal and had very strong – possibly exaggerated – feelings about "those greedy corporations" and, as much as I could use that income, I can picture her looking down on me and being very disappointed in me if I went that route.*]

A few weeks later – that is, post cocktail party confession, just as the fall semester was ending and final grades were due, I got a rather ominous summons to meet with the president of the university. I didn't know of anyone else who had ever been summoned to his office. I had a soul wrenching fear that those, who had made that trek, no longer worked here. Was the dean lying when he said they wouldn't care about the "popular" articles I had been writing? Why would the president of the university be the one to hand me a pink slip? I had met him a time or two in casual circumstances – read mostly cocktail parties – and he seemed very nice, sort of a kindly grandfather in the robes of his religious order. [*Remember, as a Catholic university the person at the top is more likely to be a defender of the faith than a business shark. Or maybe I was just projecting my hopes on the guy.*]

Chapter 2 – "Do we still have an Inquisition?'

I felt like a kid who had been called to the principal's office. Or at least what I imagined such a kid would feel like. I was always the good kid who never got in trouble, unlike the tales of some of my older brother's escapades in high school. Likewise, I hadn't ever had a reason to visit the office of the university president, and frankly I was a bit disappointed. In my imagination I had pictured an old historic building where I would walk down a dim hallway lined with the busts of scholars and famous figures out of history. At the end of the hallway, I would approach a set of huge double doors that opened into a waiting room guarded by an old, wizened attack secretary sitting at a desk that was covered with arcane and important-looking papers. [*Well, I was curious and a bit nervous because I didn't know what was going on, so I can probably be excused for imagining someplace more like Hogwarts than the rather modern office building I had just entered.]*

Anyway, I took the elevator to the fourth floor as the sign on the wall directed. And there in front of me spread a field of corporate-looking cubicles leading to the Office of the President of the University. The imagined "attack secretary" was actually a sweet young lady probably in her 20's and standing next to her desk was President Fr. Xavier himself. As I approached, he turned to the secretary and said, "Would you buzz the intercom and let him know that he's here." For a brief moment I was back to being the panicking high school kid again. "Him?" I squeaked with an embarrassingly high pitch because, whoever "him" was, it seemed he had managed to usurp Fr. Xavier's own office. I didn't think anyone on this campus outranked the university president.

"Ah, yes, Lee, I'm glad you could make it." Fr Xavier gave me a friendly handshake and then got right to the point. "An acquaintance of mine has something he needs to discuss with you, and I assured him that my office would be as secure as any place on campus. Since I have business elsewhere this afternoon, I suggested that you two meet here. Come along. I'll introduce you before I have to leave." His gentle smile soothed me a bit and managed to get my feet moving. The inside of his office didn't scream Dumbledore, but it looked dignified and cozy. Sitting, not behind the large desk, but if front of it in one of two sturdy looking side chairs, was a handsome blond-haired man – older than me but younger than Fr. Xavier. I couldn't decide if he looked stylishly European or like a casual Mafia Don.

"Dr Lee Andrews, this is Dr Gustav Richter." [*Ok, definitely European and not mafia*] Dr Richter stood to shake my hand with an unreadable grin on his face. With a nod and a quick "about face" Fr. Xavier was out of the room with no explanation of who this was or why I was there. [*I don't know the president well but that just seemed odd - like he couldn't wait to escape his own office.*] So, confused and a bit intimidated, I just stood there with what must have been a "deer-the-headlights" look on my face, not knowing what to do next.

"Have a seat." The suave stranger said with a slight accent that I couldn't place. "And, please, relax. Call me, Gus, it's less formal. I'm not with the inquisition after all."

"We still have an inquisition?" Damn, my voice had gone all squeaky again and I'm sure that my pallid, lives-in-the-library skin tone got a few shades even more pale.

"Not really, though when I'm in Rome, I do use their old offices sometimes.

I nervously chuckled at that, but paled even more, if possible, when he said, "No, that part wasn't a joke. When I'm in Rome I really do work out of some very old, out of the way space that once housed a few Medieval Inquisitors. It has electricity now and internet, but I'll be honest with you, the place still has a rather sinister feeling. I know all about you so let me introduce myself. My own background is in theoretical physics similar to yours. I work for the Vatican Observatory; the Vatican does have an observatory but don't let the name confuse you. It is really the official title covering all sorts of disciplines and research. Currently, I'm assigned to the Office of Paranormal Events."

"Paranormal Events" was not a topic I had ever dealt with. Summoning a bit of courage, that I didn't really feel, I managed to ask without the squeak this time, "So, why am I here? And why does someone from the Vatican need to talk with me?"

"At the recommendation of Dean Peltz and with the agreement of Fr Xavier, I'm here to talk about a job offer." Again, that was not something that had been on my radar. My own supervisors had recommended me for a new job. I don't even know what to make of that.

"You want me to work at the Vatican? That doesn't make any sense. I am an obscure Physics teacher and, well sometimes, I don't even make it to mass on Sunday. You must have the wrong person."

"On the contrary, you are just the right person. We have had you in our sights for quite a while now. Your research work is first rate, though just a bit outside the mainstream sometimes. But your other writings are what really interested us, 'Andy'. You seem comfortable dealing with the unexplained and willing to entertain some ideas that many of your fellow academics resist."

"So, let me get this straight. The VATICAN wants to hire ME to research UNEXPLAINED MYSTERIES for them?"

"Not exactly." And there was that smirk again. "First of all. you would not be working directly for the Vatican, but we would hope that you might cooperate with us on some topics of mutual interest. Second, we don't need you to do paranormal research. We are interested in you because of your own interest in Unidentified Ariel Phenomena or as they used to call them, UFOs. It won't be your mission to find out if they exist. They do and the church has known about them for a long time. Did you know that it was Pius XII who warned the US government about UFOs? If we reach an agreement today, I can share some of that data with you - on a need-to-know basis of course." His smirk seemed friendlier this time or maybe I was just getting used to it.

As I slowly recovered from that information overload, I just stared at the rug for a minute that seemed like hours. The first thought in my head was not exactly profound. It was something like, why would the Vatican have UFO files? Instead, I blurted out, "Are you joking? Am I being pranked for some reason?" Richter's smirk now became more of a grimace.

"I know this is a bit unexpected. [*'a bit?' he says*, try *'bombshell'*] Let your breathing return to normal and just listen. That's better. Do you need a glass of water - or bourbon? I think Fr. Xavier has some hidden in his desk. No? OK, then, let me explain a few things – things that will make sense once all the pieces are set in front of you. By the way, this conversation is the equivalent of one of your government's non-disclosure situations. Of course, the church won't threaten to kill you like your government might. We'll just remind you of the fires of hell reserved for those who would break what is essentially a sacred vow. [*I've gone pale again*] If you are ok with that, just nod and I'll go on." I nod. *[I think]*

"The Vatican has concluded that our planet has been visited - loosely translating the Latin - by "others not from this world" for a very long time. Certainly, some stories from the Old Testament could be interpreted that way. Ancient tales from other world religions and cultures probably witness those same experiences. The frequency seems to have increased with the passage of the ages, but it may just be that it has become easier to record and report on our visitors. In the Middle East and Western Europe, a stabilizing force for the last two millennia has been the church.

Conquerors and kings, dictators and presidents, come and go rather quickly on the stage of history and their interests are generally more practical and political. They want to gain and stay in power, and they aren't very interested in speculating about powers that are so far beyond their own control.

On the other hand, the church is all about trying to understand the world, how it works, how we fit in to it and into the grander scheme of God's universe. Also, imagine that you are a peasant who just witnessed something unexplainable and frightening, would you be more likely to talk with current civil officials - who seem just as unenlightened as you yourself -- or would you hand the information over to trusted spiritual leaders and let them ponder it?

Nod, if you are following me. [*This time, I am sure that I did.*]

So, for centuries, the church has gathered and sorted and contemplated all this material about "the others." We probably know at least as much as any of the major governments. Nevertheless, our goals are very different. Civil governments and corporations want to exploit their findings for power and wealth. And they want to cover them up for the same reasons. The church, however, is more interested in who the "others" are, what they want and, most importantly, how we can explain all this to the faithful without them losing their basic faith."

There is a pause while I try to digest all this - though it feels like I've just been fed the whole Thanksgiving turkey in one gulp. "Ok, I guess all that makes sense, but where do I fit in? Is someone offering me a job or not? My creditors won't be interested in just writing off my debts even if it's for a noble cause or the good of mankind."

"We do know about your financial situation and how you ended up that way. Dean Peltz and Fr. Xavier were both concerned that your debt issues might hold you back from seriously considering my offer. I think we can help you while you help us. Let me give you some context first.

About two months ago on a highway in the mountains of Utah on a "dark and stormy night" [*I groan at his Peanuts reference, but he just continues*] a car went off the road and the driver was severely injured. The good news is that the driver was found and taken to a nearby hospital but the bad news – sort of – is that he died during the night. ["sort of" I say out loud with a cringe] Yes, his death was awful but not just that. Don't we believe that God can bring good things out of even a bad situation? Well, the good part is how this leads to you – not that you caused the accident but that all of us might benefit from the consequences. [*I'm a little hung up on someone's death being just "sort of" a bad thing, but I'm still listening*]

You probably didn't hear about that accident because filming for the season had already wrapped up and somehow it didn't make national news. The deceased was Dr. Ambrose - "Rosy" to fans - Saint-David who was one of the researchers and on-screen personalities for the very popular show, "Alien Encounters."

"Wait, 'Rosy' is dead? How did I miss that? I loved him on that show. Alien Encounters is one of my few guilty pleasures that I watch every week. It won't be the same." For a moment I am more sad than nervous.

After letting that sink in, Gus continues. "No, it won't be the same, but it could be better because we would like you to take his place." I am back in stunned silence mode but eventually manage to mumble something that sounds like, "how is that... I don't even... I've never." Granted, it wasn't very coherent, but Gus got the gist of what I was saying. [*You would think that a college professor could be more articulate but for this conversation I don't think I'm doing too badly*.]

"By a great coincidence – or perhaps the grace of God – the producer tasked with finding Dr. Saint-David's replacement for the show happens to be an old school chum of Fr. Xavier.

With your agreement, of course, Fr. Xavier will recommend you for that position and, along with all your sterling credentials, will come a glowing recommendation from a very, very highly placed source at the Vatican.

"Are you that Vatican source? No offense, but why would you have such a big influence on him? I'm guessing that hardly anyone knows that your agency or department even exists, and I get the feeling that you would like to keep it that way." [*Finally, I can speak coherent sentences again!*]

"Oh, no, it won't be from me. The recommendation would come from someone much…much…much higher. Someone that no good, or even bad, Catholic - like Fr Xavier's producer friend – would dare ignore."

"Wait!! Are you talking about the pope? [*He is smirking again.*] THE POPE KNOWS MY NAME?"

"Please stop shouting. You will disturb that nice secretary and attract way too much attention to our meeting here. No, the pope doesn't know you by name …yet, but he is very much personally interested in what my office is doing, and he will definitely, but quietly, support this effort.

Now, you have heard my basic proposal, and I'll need your answer before I can fill you in on more of the details and what we hope you can do for us. Unfortunately, I'm going to need your answer now since a lot of factors need to be worked out and filming the new season will start next month."

I'm shocked by everything I've just heard, but I'm excited about this opportunity to work on something I've only fantasized about. I wish my life wasn't such a mess right now. "Gus" is waiting patiently for me to collect my thoughts [and some color to return to my face]. Honestly, I want to do it, but there are so many "details" in my own life to work out. Taking a calming breath, I force my brain out of 'papal fanboy mode' and into the 'practical scientist' framework so I can figure some things out. I have questions - important questions, at least to me.

"I need a few more answers or specifics before I can agree to all this. Is the university letting me go? Am I just quitting and losing all the time I have put in toward tenure? Is this new job going to pay a lot more money? You know my financial problems and I suspect that this new position won't leave me much time for writing the stuff that made me a few extra bucks – at least not at first. Am I also working for the Vatican? How will that play out and how much do you guys pay? I'm sorry to sound so mercenary but in good conscience I need to pay my lawful debts – and not get in trouble with the law. Oh, and if I agree to this will the people on the show know that I am "serving two masters?"

"Hmmm. Those are all good questions and, providentially [*slight smirk at the word play*], I have anticipated most of them. Here is what I have lined up so far. President Xavier assured me that the university will put you on indefinite leave of absence and, if you want, you can later just pick up where you left off here. No, that position on Alien Encounters doesn't pay that much more than your salary here, at least for your first season. You will not technically be working for the Vatican; you will be more of an unpaid consultant. However, and this is a big however, out of gratitude for your assistance, we will arrange for one of the Vatican's wealthier patrons to pay off all your current debts, your school loans, and your mom's medical bills. [*I think I just gasped*] Finally, the people associated with the show will not know of our arrangement or my involvement in procuring the position for you. However, I will be your point of contact. In my capacity as an "visiting professor" from Europe, I have occasionally served as a consultant the past few seasons. I will continue in that role and, since it will be obvious that we have several interests and theories in common, it will not seem unusual for us to exchange information and keep in contact."

I'm sure I'll have a thousand more questions, but I felt satisfied for now - sort of. I had never been the risk-taker in the family, but I don't have any family left and this is, without a doubt, a once-in-a-lifetime opportunity. Besides the church is asking me to do this; that has got to count for something. Shouldn't this be seen as divine guidance or a blessing in disguise? It should, but it still scares the hell out of me. On the other hand, what sort of researcher would I be if I wasn't willing to challenge the unknow? [*That sounds very brave in my head, but I'm not sure that is really me. Maybe I'm just kidding myself about a fearless commitment to scholarship. Maybe I'm still just that geeky kid building rockets in the garage, filled with dreams of starships and aliens. I think it's time to find out who I am. I have to know, one way or the other.*]

"I'll take the job." May God have mercy on my soul.

[This email arrived at me office a day later.]

From: Dr Gustav Richter

To: Dr Lee Andrews

Topic: Details on your new position

Since you are already a fan, I assume you know some basics about the show, Alien Encounters. It has been on the air for three seasons. Each season they travel to locations around the globe to places with recent UAP activity. They report on three or four encounters each season; no one ever hears about the locations that turned out to be fake or alien no-shows. There is a main team that is regularly seen on screen and a much larger support crew behind the scenes. You will be replacing Dr Ambrose Saint-David who was their resident "hard science" guy. Before the show he worked for NASA. He had a dry sense of humor and was often a guest on talk shows. Your own background is physics, and your articles often display a similar sense of humor. You should be able to comfortably be his replacement.

The team leader is Steven George. His background is computers and gaming. He was instrumental in getting the show on the air and is the final authority about production decisions. The oldest member of the team is Arthur Doyle. He has doctorates in both history and archeology. He has published over a dozen books with the most recent on "lost civilizations" making the best seller list. Shannon Timmons is the team's expert on biology. She had worked for several bio-tech companies before joining Alien Encounters. Thomas "Tesla" Williams is the show's electronics and internet guru. He is responsible for the exotic gear that they use for their alien hunting; some of it he has designed himself. He is probably the 'geekiest' of the primary team.

Steven knows that I have investigated several paranormal events and uses me as a consultant. I do not appear on screen, but I frequently join them for the alien-hunting excursions. They have about a 75% success rate in spotting and recording UAP – 90% of which are saucers and 10% the more elusive glowing orbs. Steven plans to move beyond just observing the coming season. At the moment, I don't know what that entails.

Vatican data has detected a spike in alien encounters over the last five years, specifically with the saucer types and those sightings are lengthier and sometimes more intrusive than past events. We aren't ready for people to know the extent to which the Vatican is interested in UAP or aliens. Too many people still doubt their existence and it would damage our credibility. I will send you that data and some past reports in a separate email for your eyes only. Though I will not be on site all the time, but I will be there frequently and serve as your contact with the Vatican. You have my private phone number should you need to reach me.

A final reminder; as far as the team and crew know we have never met; keep that in mind when we are introduced.

Chapter 3 – "Introductions and rubber chicken"

An ominous looking flying saucer came into view then flared into a brilliant orange light. That's how the enormous flat screen at the front of the room came to life with the teaser for the upcoming season of Alien Encounters. Then followed a montage of alien creatures too fast to see clearly. A few seconds of silence and then we see a lonely planet Earth floating in the dark emptiness of endless space. The image is captured from maybe about twice the distance of the lunar orbit - subtly implying that someone is looking down on us with a view we don't usually see. As the picture of the earth slowly grows, the voice of Steven George, our head producer and big boss, begins to remind everyone of the wonders that faithful viewers shared last season. "We have seen strange phenomena and recorded the impact of their appearance.

We have even found some techniques that seem to encourage their presence. [pictures of lots of scientific looking equipment flash by] This season we will try everything at our disposal to get them to interact with us, possibly even communicate with us. We could be at the dawn of a new understanding of our place in the universe. Check your local time and listings for the new season of Alien Encounters coming this Fall."

As the screen fades and the lights in the large conference room brighten, the real-life voice of the show's producer continues, "Welcome back to all our cast and support staff and welcome to those just joining our team as we prep for this season. We are going to keep this morning light and informal; I don't want to get into all the stuff before lunch that might ruin your digestion or give you nightmares. *[I expected a few chuckles at that comment but, ominously, there was just silence]*

It goes without saying that we deeply mourn the loss of "Rosy" Saint-David. His insights and dry British sense of humor were a treasure and will be missed. On a much happier note, welcome Dr Lee Andrews as one of our main researchers and on-screen presenters. I won't go through all his impressive credentials as a physicist, but he fills the slot of our new "Mr. Spock." [*This time there are chuckles; I'm not sure that's good*] However, some of you might also know him by his pen name. Lee has asked that we keep this among us, but he has agreed that I can tell you that he is also known as the popular writer, Andy Leland."

From the back of the room someone shouts "Oh, God, Andy Leland. I think I have read all your online stuff. I loved you article on 'Aliens: nannies or wardens?' That was a little creepy and funny as hell. We talked about that at lunch for days."

"See, Lee, you already have a fan club. [*I blush, I never had a fan club before.*] For other newcomers with the crew, let me just quickly introduce the main team. You have just met Lee; next to him is Shannon Timmons, our biologist and, in case of an emergency, a trained EMT; then Arthur Doyle, our archeologist and history buff; and finally, Thomas "Tesla" Williams, our guru for all things electronic. [Steven pauses for polite applause]

There are a couple of other folk I should introduce. Some of you have already met this guy occasionally over the last few seasons. Dr. Gus Richter is a consultant on loan to us from the Vatican Observatory; his background is astrophysics but now he mostly dabbles in all things spooky or weird."

Gus pipes up to add, "Let's just call them "odd phenomena." As you say, we don't want to scare people before lunch. [Why is no one laughing about those comments referring to scary stuff? That definitely moves to the top of my growing list of questions.]

"Finally," Steven continues, "I need to introduce the two big guys that I am sure you have noticed standing by the door as you came into the room. They are obviously identical twins; they are Peter and Paul Kowalski, our new heads of security. They did tell me that they prefer to go by their code names of "Rambo" – in the black uniform – who will monitor the physical security of our operations, and "Spook" who will oversee cybersecurity and intel procedures – he will typically be the one in casual clothes. We do have a few other support staff who are new, but rather than drag this out you can all just mingle and introduce yourselves at lunch. Let's take a leisurely two hours. Support staff will then coordinate with their supervisors here in this large conference room while the main research team plus Gus, Rambo and Spook will meet with me in the small conference room near my office."

The catered lunch wasn't quite ready to serve so people were all mingling around the cafeteria, just as Steven suggested, getting acquainted with the newbies, or reacquainted with work buddies from last season. I noticed Gus at the far end of the room. He never looked my way, yet when we finally did sit down to eat, he somehow ended up sitting right next to me. He doesn't exactly ignore me, but he is very good at not letting on that we know each other. As the salads are served, I turn to him and ask – like any typical stranger would – "So, the Vatican Observatory, you must be interested in astronomy, that doesn't seem spooky or weird?"

A bit condescendingly, as a stranger might do, he explains, "No, I do work in theoretical physics and paranormal phenomena. The Vatican does have an observatory, but the name covers a whole range science and research departments. It has long been the position of the church that faith and reason, science and belief, don't contradict but reinforce each other. If science clearly tells us something, then we work to see how it fits into our worldview in the light of our faith. That can lead us in a lot of different directions including the paranormal and alien encounters."

Somehow Gus manages to sound like he is reading from prepared lecture notes. I'm not sure if that is part of his disguise or he just likes to sound authoritative.

I haven't learned everybody's name yet but one of our other lunch table companions interjects, "Don't you have to do a lot of adjusting to that worldview, Dr Richter? You know stuff like creation in seven days or samples of every animal in one boat."

"If I were a stubborn fundamentalist, you would be correct. But I'm not, and neither is my church. Some of our greatest scientists are believers who say the wonders of science just point more strongly to the mysteries of the divine. But you know what? This is way too heavy of a conversation to have over what looks to be rubber chicken and mashed potatoes. So, different topic now. Lee, I have read a few of your articles. You can be quite entertaining while sticking close to some pretty good science. Are you still going to keep writing that sort of thing?"

Chewing my rubber chicken thoughtfully, I answer, "I don't know. I don't know how much spare time I'll have now, and I need to check with the legal department about what sort of things are covered by that non-disclosure paperwork. Have you written anything I should read?"

Gus had wisely given up on the rubber chicken, but after continuing to move the mashed potatoes around his plate for a few seconds, he responds. "I like to keep a low profile and my bosses at the Vatican might not take kindly to any speculations that might seem too out of the ordinary. Not that people at the Vatican can't speculate, it's just that we don't like to get into messy public disagreements with our more famous colleagues. We have too much to do without that distraction. On the other hand, I would like to chat with you about some of your own work. It's not always the mainstream approach and I find that refreshing."

I hope a light bulb didn't just appear above my head. I realized that Gus had publicly established a reason for us to get together and talk that would not seem suspicious for two people who had supposedly just met. Damn, he is really good at this clandestine stuff. Maybe his nickname should be Spook. We did agree to get together sometime soon and then he skillfully turned to chat with the others at our table for the rest of the meal. [*James Bond, eat your heart out.*]

[Personal Journal – Entry #1

I never kept a diary before. I tended to think of diaries as something where angst ridden teenagers or people with low self-esteem could rewrite the script of their lives giving themselves a starring role. Since I find myself starting this record, I'll have to assume that my previous opinion was flawed. I'm writing this because my life is moving very fast right now and I don't want to lose track of anything important. This entry will be short, I'm just killing a few minutes after the lunch that didn't take two hours.

I can't believe I am working on my favorite tv show; it all happened so fast. Surprisingly, I haven't felt homesick for the university. I certainly don't miss that shabby dump of an apartment I had been living in. The university was very gracious considering my hasty departure. The move here went smoothly; I didn't really have much to move beyond the books in my office and some clothes. The cheap furniture all stayed with the nasty apartment.

The studio helped me find a nice apartment in a good section of town and, for maybe the first time in my life, I felt unburdened, free. All my debts were paid off, I had a job that both seemed exciting and paid well. I even received a "relocation

bonus." I secretly wonder if Gus's fingerprints are on that, but Steven says it was because I was able to move in such short time to help fill out the team. This is great! So why do I keep waiting for the other shoe to drop?]

After lunch, Rambo and Spook – the real one, not Gus – helped me find the small conference room where the core staff would be meeting. Once I got over being intimidated by the twin brutes' size, I found out that they were very cordial and easy to talk with. I'm about average size but the twins were at least 6'5" or 6'6" and solid muscle. Honestly, they looked more like bouncers at a bar or renegade super soldiers than staff for a TV program. I wondered what they had been doing before they came to work here but we had just met and I didn't want to pry…yet.

We found our way to a windowless conference room where the rest of the primary team were already sitting quietly –

maybe too quietly. The easygoing chatter over lunch was nowhere to be found. Our head producer, Steven George, entered and went straight to the podium at the front of the room and then looked up at the twins who were again standing by the door like sentries. With a serious tone that said that this was way more than a business meeting, he asked them, "Are we ready to begin?"

Almost with a salute, Spook shouts, "Yes, sir, Rambo will be standing guard outside the door. Once I press the button on this remote, this room will be as electronically secure as the Pentagon's war room."

That other shoe just dropped.

Chapter 4 – Behind Closed Doors

At the press of a different button, a screen behind Steven lit up with a list of bullet points. Great, in addition to the over-the-top security measures, we were now faced with "death by PowerPoint." [*In a flashback to the university, I wonder how often did my students feel oppressed by the endless slides of doom? They were right. Karma is a bitch. PowerPoint slides are like good whisky. A reasonable amount can be very helpful, but too much can mess you up.*] But enough daydreaming, I was here now, and I needed to pay special attention because I was the new guy on the block. Even so, I do feel confident that I can make a contribution to this team. I am not a stranger to the world of UAP and "little green men," after all, that's what most of my money-making articles were about. Even my more academic writings would often allude to the possible physics of such phenomena. As Steven joked this morning, I find myself filling the "Science Officer" spot on this team and I need to assure them they chose wisely in hiring me. [*Though I'm going to have to avoid the temptation to say, "live long and prosper."*]

"Alright, as you can see, we have a lot to cover this afternoon," Steven intones in that same serious voice that he used on this morning's promotional video. "We are doing this review partially to see if Lee has questions or input that we need to deal with and partially to make sure we are all starting the season on the same page. Then the rest of the week we will gather here to scope out and refine what's planned for the coming season. [*Wait, did he just blame this meeting on 'the new guy?' So, this is what the underside of the bus looks like.*]

As you know we work much more "in the field" than in this studio. We will travel to several locations that show heightened UAP activity, and those destinations can change quickly if a new, more interesting one pops up. The last few seasons have shown that these events have a lot of common properties, but we never know exactly what to expect – we have been surprised in the past – so the more contingency planning we do now, the less scrambling we will have to do in the field. I'll start off asking Arthur for a Readers Digest overview of UAP history and legends. Arthur."

"I'm going to skip over lots of stuff but stop me if you have questions. Our distant ancestors left us stories of gods who descended from the heavens in flaming craft. Maybe they did shoot fire, as our own rockets do, but since fire was their only known light source, they could just be describing these vehicles as glowing. Firey flying chariots were mostly the standard description. These ancestors seem to claim a lot more personal interaction with these beings back then. They described the earliest of them as giants – possibly a physical description or it could be just a way to describe them as powerful. Later, the visitors were often depicted with animal-like features like you see in

Egyptian tomb paintings. Maybe that was accurate or maybe, for example, if you saw someone fly, you might explain it by showing wings and bird-like characteristics. Later cultures gave their gods less fanciful and more recognizably human form. Think of the gods of Greece, Rome, the Norsemen. There is interesting speculation that they were dealing with hybrids during that period. There is no way to verify that though reports of hybrids have become common in our own day.

For the last couple thousand years there doesn't seem to have been as much direct human/visitor personal interaction. There have always been sightings of flying objects and usually that was either what we would classify as saucer-like or as glowing balls of light - think fairies and spirit creatures. Those two – saucers and orbs - are still the most dominant form of UAP today. To that I would add the triangles – which I personally believe are human manufactured; the rather rare large cylinders – speculated to be supplies ships or command carriers; then there are the "ticktacks" that are all the rage with military sightings recently. Again, my personal feeling is that those are also human made. Except for the smaller balls of light which tend to flit about, aliens seem a bit more discrete, while these ticktacks seem like they want to show off and that strikes me as more of a human trait. And I recently saw a picture on the internet of something that looked more like cube. I don't think the Borg have arrived so I would tentatively classify that one as a fake."

Steven interrupts to ask, "who is making the human made stuff?"

"That is a great question, but I don't have an answer. Undoubtedly some of it comes from our own government research and "black ops" projects. Some may represent a more shadowy "rogue" group who may or may not work with the government as needed, but that could just be internet gossip. A group like that would need a lot of money, some place to hide their operations, and an incredible amount of secrecy that might require deadly force to impose. So, the short answer is "I don't know, and they are talking."

As a sidebar to alien craft, though I haven't researched this yet, it seems to me that the number of crashed UFO's has increased drastically in the last 50 years. Lee, you have talked about crashes in your writings. Do you see the same thing?"

[On the one hand, I have to admit it felt good to be consulted on something, and so soon in the meeting. On the other hand, I have to be careful not reveal similar information that I got from the Vatican archives.] After a few seconds collecting my thoughts I answered Arthur, "I do agree with your hunch and in one article I speculated about possible reasons for that. Partially, we might just be getting a lot better at spotting and locating crashes, but there might be factors on the alien side too. You all know that the more sophisticated your car gets, the more expensive, the more difficult it is to get repaired. Crashes might be something as

simple as metal fatigue that we see in airplanes. Crash remnants suggest that UAP are made of some very exotic metals that you just can't pick up at your local hardware; we don't even know how to make the stuff. Or, consider this, these things have been around for a very long time, and they might just be approaching the end of their warranty. Maybe even more significant is that **we** have become increasingly high tech in the last century and some of that tech may interfere with their propulsion or navigation systems. That is something we here on the show might need to be careful about as we make increasingly aggressive attempts to reach out to them."

At that point Steven says, "OK, let's take a quick 10-minute break."

[Personal Journal Entry #2

I am feeling pretty good so far. There wasn't anything in Arthur's summary that I hadn't already encountered, and he asked me a question to which I could give a coherent answer. Yay, me! Of course, this is still more of an academic exercise for me. Unlike the rest of the team, I haven't personally encountered a UAP of any sort yet. Part of me can't wait for that to happen... and part of me is curled up in a little ball saying that I am very comfortable just waiting, thank you.]

After the break Steven takes the lead again, "If there are no immediate questions, I'll turn this over to Shannon, our biologist, to recap some views on the visitors behind all these UAP. Shannon, the floor is yours."

"You may have heard the internet darling, Ryan Greer, claim that there something like 80 different species of alien. There may be true, but most likely the odds of them all showing up here on our little planet seem very small. So, I'll winnow this down to the ones that have been consistently reported.

Like Arthur said, the most common vehicle is the saucer and the alien most associated with that is the 'gray' – or "grey" as Rosy used to prefer. You have all seen the various images: small, thin body; large head, huge eyes – a guaranteed nightmare for children everywhere. The government won't admit it, but any "biologic" found at crash sites could most likely be classified as grays. Unfortunately, we don't have direct access to that data. The stuff on the internet is interesting but not solid enough for us to draw conclusions that we could present on the show.

However, and this is strictly just between us, they seem to have a similar basic biology to us since they breathe our air and seem comfortable enough hanging around in our environment. Are they our genetic ancestors or maybe our descendants? That's what some people claim. I don't know. Their spindly bodies seem more adapted to life in space than in the gravity well of a planet and that tends to suggest that they are a very, very old race. If we can believe abduction reports, they seem to use telepathy to communicate. With that in mind,

Steven, we might need to include a respected psychic on our team in future attempts to establish communication. [*That didn't seem to get much of a response from Steven, so I didn't say anything though it sounded like a good idea to me. I'm the new guy and it sounded like this topic had come up before.*]

Moving along. Far less common, and so, far less understood, there are some infrequent encounters with a few other types. There are the reptilians and sometimes they too are associated with saucer-like craft. There are the taller, fury ones that are quite rare and usually just written off as sasquatches - whatever they are. Then there are some associate beings. People have reported seeing what looked like alien human hybrids and, of course, the favorites of tv's X Files, there are the notorious "men in black." They sound very much like the ones referred as Nordics, who are very pale, usually white haired and having "odd eyes." The difference would be the men in black seem to have much better tailers and favor snappy black suits.

I have all sorts of fun speculations that we can chat about over lunch someday but for now I've given you the more commonly accepted views on our visitors. If you ever catch one, find me. I'll grab my scalpel and come running." [*I hope she is kidding; dissections are a terrible way to make friends.*]

"Thank you, Shannon, for ending with that rather disturbing image. Any questions for her? Yes, Lee, go ahead."

"Orbs. Alive or not? We seemed to skip over them."

Shannon isn't exactly stumped but paused for a significant moment. "Their actions seem sometimes purposeful and sometimes playful. That reminds me of a living organism but their speed, acceleration, movements would be very stressful on any biologic that we are familiar with. So, I'll give you a very definite maybe."

Taking the podium again, Steven says, "We've reviewed some of the material that we have discovered or gathered – there are lots of fascinating scenarios. But you also know that we have never come close to presenting anything like that on the show so far. I think we all need to be clear about our limitations. We're going to talk about that here in our locked, secure room – but only here. And there are at least four good reasons why we have to be careful about what goes on the air. There are…forces…that would be most unhappy to have us go public with all this.

First, there are our own government politicians. They have their own agendas and don't want anyone suggesting that there are more important things to consider. We can push them along a little, but we have to do it tactfully.

Then there is what is called the "deep state." These are the life-long bureaucrats who know where all the black money comes from and where it really goes. They don't want to be exposed and in many ways are more powerful than the politicians. We will try to avoid them if possible.

Next, there is a smaller group. Once upon a time President Dwight Eisenhower called them the "military industrial complex." Now people on the web timidly refer to them as "the rogues." They are the ones who reverse-engineer alien salvage and then use it for their own nefarious purposes – think the triangle UFO and the ticktacks. Sometimes they work for or with the government and sometimes they don't. They would be the most secretive and probably the most dangerous. Let's hope we don't have to deal with them.

Having laid out the cautions, I have to tell you, however, that this season will be different. We are going to be more aggressive in our tactics and more transparent about what goes on the air. We can't keep just hinting season after season at the things we have discovered. "Rosy" Saint-David had been chomping at the bit to expose our findings, and I plan to honor his memory by doing just that, when it is reasonably safe to do so. [*I just had a terrible feeling that Dr. Saint-David's accident wasn't so accidental. I can't tell if anyone else had the same thought, so again I'll keep it to myself for now.*]

There is one last factor to consider, our viewing audience. They are curious and faithful as long as we don't confuse them or scare them. Like the politicians they elect, they don't want their comfy little worlds disturbed by "the bigger picture." The bottom line for us is self-preservation. We want to be brave and honest but if we go too far or too fast, they will change the channel. The show will go belly up and our research will lose all its funding.

That sums up the balancing act we will be facing this season and I know it won't be simple. I'm counting on your advice, your insight, and your discretion to make this work. I know that was kind of a downer note to end on but our planning the rest of the week needs to balance the new territory we want to explore with the need to proceed with caution."

Glancing at the clock, he continues," I don't know about you but it's getting late, and I need to be home for dinner. We'll call it a day and I'll see you tomorrow."

As the group breaks up, I stop Shannon for a minute for a quick "orb" question. Her answer is interrupted by a loud growl from my empty stomach – I just couldn't eat that rubber chicken at lunch. Looking around I see everyone else has gone, so I ask Shannon if she would like to get some supper with me. [*This is me following my resolution to be more outgoing and social.*]

"Thanks, may some other time; I've busy tonight." And with a wink and a smile she is out the door. [*This is me feeling rejected.*]

However, from that door, Spooks says, "As soon as Rambo finishes clearing the building, we are heading out to get some grub. You want to come with us?"

"Sounds good to me. I don't really know the area yet and I don't like to go to a restaurant alone. Let's go." By the time we get to the lobby,

Rambo is waiting for us. After we leave the building, Spook touches a nearly invisible panel near the door. He presses a few buttons, lights flash green, and he announces that we are ready to go.

As we climb into the twins absurdly huge SUV, Rambo asks, "Lee, are you ok with Mexican? There is a great little hole-in-the-wall place nearby. They have decent prices, serve huge quantities and it's even pretty good."

As my stomach rumbled one more time, I told him. "You had me with huge quantities."

Chapter 5 – Big Brother is watching.

The food was good, and I had been hungry, but I was astounded at how much each of the twins could put away. They turned out to be good dinner companions and time flew by as we got to know each other better. I found out that they had been doing security work as a team for years. It could be standard with security professionals, but they were evasive about their previous jobs. They just said that they came to work for the studio because they needed a change of scenery. There has got to be more to that story but that was all I was going to get tonight. As we headed out of the restaurant, I reached into my front pocket and found it empty. It dawned on me that in my stomach-grumbling haste to grab some food, I left my keys in my briefcase and my briefcase in the conference room. "Guys, I don't mean to imply anything, but could you break into my apartment for me? My keys are back at the studio, and I know you locked it up for the night as we were leaving."

A big grin lit up Rambo's face, "We appreciate your confidence in our ability to do questionably legal acts, but there is an easier solution. Spook, can you handle that for Lee?

"Sure can. Lee, you do have your security badge with you, don't you?

"Yes, I remember that being emphasized by HR when I was in processed for the job. It was a little corny, but it stuck. 'This badge is your friend; it gets lonely if it isn't with you so always have it on hand.' It's in my shirt pocket, because I also remember being told not to wear it out in public."

"Hand it to me so I can get the code numbers off of it." I pass it to Spook who is now tapping something on what appears to be a smartphone. After he enters my badge code, he hands it back and taps some more. When the gadget makes a happy little chirp, Spook turns to me in the back seat and instructs, "Be sure you clip the badge to the front of your shirt. We will drop you off in front of the studio. Go to the main doors at the lobby entrance. Tap the badge against the little black square to the left of the double doors. The doors will unlock to let you in, and the badge will give you access to the conference room where we have been meeting. Is your car in the back parking lot? [I nod] Ok, you don't have to leave through the lobby doors. After you get your stuff, you can go out through the door near the parking lot. The badge will let you out without setting off any alarms."

"Wow, I didn't realize our building security was so high tech."

"It's not." says Rambo with a little disgust in his voice. "You should see the really good stuff, but that's not in the budget right now so for the immediate future we have to make do with what we have."

We pulled up in front of the studio. I thanked the twins for their help and wave as they burn rubber on their way down the street to fight crime or rescue kittens or whatever super soldiers like them do with their free time. [*Yes, that super soldier fantasy is still lurking in my imagination.*] With all the windows and security lighting, it's easy to move through the lobby. As I move deeper into the building where there are no windows and only the glow of the occasional exit signs for lighting, it gets harder to see in the hallways. But I am familiar with the layout of the building by now and I don't have much further to go. Even as a kid I don't remember being afraid of the dark and I can always use the flashlight on my phone if it gets too murky.

Just as I'm feeling smug about my bravery, I turn the last corner and run smack into an obstacle that shouldn't be there. The obstacle is warm and flexible and even before I can mumble an appropriate obscenity, it has me pinned against the wall with a strong arm against my chest and a gloved hand firmly clamped on my mouth. There is enough light that I can see that the obstacle is a man dressed all in black and wearing a matching black ski mask. We just stare at each other for what seems like an unusual amount of time. Then my ninja cat burglar shakes his head and whispers to himself what sounded like, "It had to be you."

After some more very uncomfortable staring, ninja asks quietly, "Are you alone? [*I nod, I seem to do a lot of nodding in awkward situations*] If you promise not to call for help and not to try to run away, I'll take my hand off your mouth and stop smashing you into the wall. Deal?"

I know you aren't supposed to make deals with terrorists because you can't trust them, and it just encourages them to continue their evil ways. I'm not sure about the protocol for ninja cat burglars. Clearly this guy could have already hurt me if he wanted to, and it would be nice to feel less squished against the wall like a bothersome bug. So, I nod [*of course*] and ninja guy take a step back. What happened next is a plot twist worthy of Steven King. The guy reaches up and removes his ski mask so I can see his face. [*In the movies that usually means they have decided to kill you, I pray this is a different movie.*] Now I was the one who stared. If I were a Southern belle, I would have swooned but what I actually did was come at him with my best punch right to the face. But he caught my hand in mid-punch, just like he always did when we were kids.

"Daniel? I thought you were dead."

"Lee, I thought you were a nerdy science teacher."

There were a million things I could have asked at that point, but I am a bit ashamed to say that my first instinct was to be petty and spiteful, so I went right to something not at all helpful to this current situation.

"You didn't even come to mom's funeral."

"I couldn't.

You guys didn't even hold a memorial service for me."

[*Ok, that's a fair come-back. I guess that being-spiteful instinct is a family trait.*] "We couldn't. Mom always held on to the hope you would come back. A memorial would have been too final for her."

Looking around cautiously, Daniel suggests, "This corridor is not the place for a family reunion and there are definitely some things we have to discuss."

"No kidding. OK, I have access to the small conference room that is right around the corner and its…"

"Secure. I know."

Chapter 6 – Something Special

[Daniel - About 10 ten years ago]

I was graduating with honors from high school next week. I had a wall covered with awards and trophies; I could have had a scholarship for my athletic ability. I had several offers, but I turned them all down and never told my folks about it. My little brother was the genius in the family; he was college material. That kid could sit and read books all day long and be happy as a clam. On the other hand, I think of myself as restless and adventuresome; though Lee calls me reckless and cocky. He's probably right. I love the little shit, but we don't have much in common other than having the same mom and dad. These days we rarely even cross paths that much expect those times when we fight over space in the garage. I want to use the garage to work on my old motorcycle – who knows, someday I might even get to run. Lee wants to be in there to build his model rockets and I have to admit that he is having a lot more success with his hobby than I am with mine.

I put off discussing my future plans with my parents as long as possible, but eventually the topic couldn't be avoided any longer. Can you be surprised, but not surprised? The was sort of the reaction from my folks when I informed them that I had signed up to join the Army and would be leaving for basic training at Fort Benning in Georgia not long after graduation. I expected something different; I was ready to do battle, but they had already surrendered. They didn't try to get me to reconsider college; they didn't say I was making a mistake. It was like their expectations for me were realistically subdued.

When it came time to go, there would be the mandatory tearful goodbyes and promises to write, call, and visit home whenever I could. I think I honestly meant those promises, but it wasn't long before they faded from my mind. I lost myself in being away from home and doing something that I really wanted to do instead of what was expected of me.

A lot of recruits did nothing but complain about their new military life. Not me; I loved it, and it turns out I was really good at it – so good that in an astonishingly short period of time I was encouraged to sign up for Special Ops. And that was even better. It was training on steroids and the thrill of secret missions and clandestine operations. I'm not bragging, but this felt like what I was born for. It was perfect for me, and I couldn't imagine anything better. Until something better knocked on my door.

The chain of command noticed that I had a real talent for special ops, so I started to get picked more often for what I thought of as special, special ops. These are tricky situations where secrecy is paramount, and things could turn deadly in a heartbeat. There was one particularly rough mission that involved rescuing a bunch of missionaries from a ruthless African warlord who threaten to torture them one-by-one unless he was paid some absurd ransom and guaranteed immunity for all his horrendous deeds. It turned out that one of the missionaries was a nephew of a very prominent Washington Cabinet Secretary. There were a lot of military brass watching over this one and in spite of all the smooth operations my unit had handled before, this was the one where everything seemed to go wrong.

Other than two of us who had been scouting ahead, the rest of rescue team had been captured and one of the missionaries had already suffered a nearly fatal beating. This is where being fearless – or stupidly reckless – came in handy. While the other ops guy went to find help, I, under the cover of darkness, crawled for hours to sneak into the warlord's compound. Honestly, I wasn't totally crazy. The mercenaries thought they had captured all the rescue team, giving them the prize of even more hostages to bargain for or just torture for the fun of it. As a result, the warlord and his men were celebrating and by the time I got there, they were knock down, flat on their ass, drunk.

It took while but I managed to locate the warlord's room - because of the two guards that had passed out in front of his door.

Warning: The next part is not for the faint of heart and thankfully never made into the official after-action report. Stepping over the useless guards, I entered the room to find the big bad guy himself – also passed out drunk and curled up in the fetal position, naked on this bed. I had a few essential medical supplies with me, so I gave him a shot that would keep him unconscious for at least a few more hours and started to work on my plan. I gagged him and stretched him out spread eagle on the bed and securely tied him into that position face up. [*I know what you are thinking and, NO, I am not into BDSM, but the situation was desperate, and I didn't have many options for getting all of us out of here.*] I then proceeded to cut off his left thumb.

After that, I quickly dressed the wound, so he wouldn't bleed to death – I needed him alive, and preferably distracted by pain, for this to work. I taped the dismembered thumb to his chest where it would be clearly seen and then I maneuvered myself so that I was sitting behind him on the bed. Yep, I know it sounds like creepy porn again but with him against my chest as protection I wasn't such an easy target for his men. Knife in hand I sat and waited for his hungover troops to crawl into the sunlight of a new day.

From that point it went unexpectedly smoothly. When the first guard came into the room, I made it clear that any wrong moves and his boss was dead. I had already assured his evilness, the warlord, that unless he ordered his men to do what I had instructed, I planned to cutoff something that he would miss a lot more than a thumb. [Use your imagination folks] The hostages and my team were quickly loaded onto two trucks for their departure. I then placed a device between the warlord's legs that I told him was a small charge of C4 with both motion sensor and remote detonation capabilities. It was really just the small pouch were had I carried my medical supplies, but it sounded like a believable thing that evil Americans might carry – and let's face it these guys are not very bright and still not thinking too clearly with their hangovers in full force. I convinced them it would automatically disarm in two hours as long as no one touched the bed. I also made clear that if anyone tried to stop us, I would set it off by remote. This weird scheme should not have worked. So many things could have, probably should have, gone wrong. But Thank God and cheap liquor, we did get everyone out alive. This event brought me the attention that would change my life.

But first, I got to home base to find out that my father had just died. I made it home for the funeral, but it didn't feel like home anymore. My life was fast paced, high pressure [*and I'll admit it now, exciting and a bit addictive*]. When I look back, it saddens me because that would be the last time I came back to that little town, the last time I would see my mother alive, the last time my not so little brother would yell at me for not coming home more often and not caring about my family.

It was about 6 months after I got back to the base from my dad's funeral that a couple of very official looking gentlemen in expensive suits asked to see me. It took them a while to come to the point, but their offer was for me to move up to something even more special and secret, a position that they claimed was even "more essential to our national interests." When I asked them, they said it wasn't the FBI, CIA or NSA. In fact, they said they didn't have any initials because they were too high level to have a recognizable name. [*Maybe that should have set off alarm bells in my head, but since they were obviously here with the permission of my military superiors it seemed reasonable at the time.*]

I doubt they would have answered but I probably should have asked more questions. After that depressing trip home for the funeral, I was still out of sorts, not myself. So, it was encouraging to hear that someone really valued my work. The offer seemed like a real honor. I did ask if I would have to wait until my current enlistment was up, but they said they would take care of all the details, and I should be ready to go in about two months.

That would be a rough two months. I wanted to say goodbye to all my buddies that had really become my family for the last few years, but I couldn't tell them where I was going – I didn't even know where I was going. I didn't tell my family because that relationship was still kind of awkward. I'm sure it wasn't true, but back then I told myself they didn't even care what I was doing so why stir up more issues. That was a terrible reason not to confide in my family but in the long run it turned out to be the best choice.

I found out that my new situation was a whole level of secrecy and potential danger that I could never have imagined. And I was fine with that. I didn't really mind the prospect of intrigue or clandestine ops and I was fascinated by the months of training we went through. There were only a few of us and each of us was being prepared with slightly different specialties and new skills. I was learning about things I didn't even know were possible. Every now and then, I imagined how impressed my nerdy little brother would be if I could show him some of this material. But the more I learned about who we were and what we did, I knew that would never happen.

In fact, I eventually came to understand that if anyone ever figured out that I was involved in this, they might seek leverage over me by threatening my friends or family. I had left my few friends behind long ago, but I did still have a family. I just couldn't allow any harm to come to mom or Lee because of my choices. To protect them, I took the route that others had taken before me. Back when I started my new training, they had already been informed that I was missing but the military was still looking for me. That way they wouldn't wonder why they didn't hear from me or, worse yet, start looking for me. It was out of their hands and all they could do was trust that the government was on the case.

Soon, when I finished my training, they would hear that I was presumed dead – body never found. There would be no connection to endanger them. Because I loved them, we would never meet again.

Chapter 7 – Who doesn't love a family reunion?

Neither of us speak until, using my badge, we enter the conference room, turn on some lights and sit down at the table. Then simultaneously we say, "What the hell are you doing here?" [*Isn't it nice that brothers think so alike"*]

"I'll go first. I'm easy. I work here. Now you, and don't you dare skip over the part about why you aren't dead." I have so many emotions warring inside me – anger, suspicion, joy, sorrow, regret, and more anger – that they all cancel out and that remark came out cold as ice rather than the more neutral icebreaker I had intended. A part of me couldn't believe that my brother was sitting across the table from me. A part of me wanted to beat the hell out of the no-good bastard who had abandoned me twice – disappearing into the military and then disappearing from the face of the earth.

"Lee, I can't begin to understand what you went through, and you probably won't believe me, but I missed you more than I can say. I am so sorry that I had to leave you and mom behind.

I can still read your face, little brother, and it looks like you are holding back a string of obscenities just like the day I backed my motorcycle over your brand-new rocket. I don't blame you for feeling that way but please, let me finish then you can tell me that you hate me and wish I really were dead.

When I left home after graduation, I didn't intend to cut you guys out of my life, but I just had to get out of that stupid little town. Mom and Dad weren't thrilled, but the military was a great choice for me. I was good at it and moved up quickly. I loved what I was doing, it focused me and gave me purpose. But the part I do regret is that I let it consume me to the point where it took over my life. I shoved you guys aside – and, sadly, out of mind.

I'm not sure you remember, but by the time dad died I was in Special Ops. I had just returned from a mission where I had to do a lot of reckless and dangerous things, but I also managed to save a lot of people. I wasn't much help to you and mom when I got home. I was physically and emotionally drained from the mission, miserable that dad died before I ever got to tell him that I turned out ok, frustrated with myself for just ignoring – avoiding you – for so long. When I left after the funeral, I promised myself that I would be back and do better at caring for my family. You know how that turned out.

What you don't know is that not long after I got involved in something way beyond any missions the military could offer me. It would be covert and very dangerous at times. That's really all I can tell you and probably more than I should have told you, but I do owe you some explanation. I found out that not only was my new occupation dangerous for me but that it could be dangerous for any family or any friends connected to me. So, I had to break all my connections. To keep you and mom safe, I had to let you mourn me as dead. That's about all I can safely say about why I am not dead.

Why am I here?

I think that turns out to be a two-part question. First, you are a smart guy so I'm sure you have already figured out that the people I work for must be concerned about what your program is discovering and what you plan to do next. Why else would anyone be prowling these hallways in the dark?

The second part is more complicated. Originally the plan was to get me placed in some grunt job on the staff so I could hang around and see what was going on. That plan went to hell when I was stunned to learn that my little brother was somehow involved in the project. I knew that if you spotted me, you would recognize me for sure, blow my cover and totally expose my mission. That would be bad for me and possibly very bad for you.

The other alternative was to break in, look through files and computers and hopefully plant some very discrete bugs throughout the studio. I might be able to find out what was being planned and, with the building empty, you could never discover me. So, I made sure that everyone had gone home for the evening, and no one was in the building. I needed to do this undetected and, mostly, I needed to not run into you. And again, you know how that turned out.

Now it's your turn again, Lee. What the hell are you doing here tonight - or at all?"

After I heard Daniel's story, I felt sad and full of regrets for lost years; I wasn't so angry anymore. So, in fair trade I would give him a civil two-part answer. "You're right. I was teaching physics at a small mid-western university. I liked academic life – and I was good at that. But with grad school loans and caring for mom – without your help [*Yeah, apparently, I am more bitter about that than I wanted to admit to myself*] – I found myself buried under a mountain of debt, and I wasn't digging myself out. To bring in some extra cash I started writing non-academic pieces for magazines and blogs under a pen name. It wasn't much but it did give me a bigger shovel to dig with. However, those articles attracted the attention of some people who turned out to be very good friends who recommended me to replace Ambrose Saint-David when he died a few months ago in a car accident. "

"YOU replaced Saint-David?" Daniel erupts. " Oh, my God, I'm getting sloppy, I should have followed up on that. It's my fault that you are mixed up in all this! [*I think the neutral listening-face that I was working on just turned sour.*]

No, wait, don't jump to conclusions. I didn't kill him. Swear as my brother that you never tell this to another living soul. [*guess what, I nod*] Ambrose isn't dead... probably. It was my job to stage that crash. My people took him to a hospital so the authorities could verify it was him. During the night we snuck him out and replaced him with a dead body from the city morgue. The hospital night crew didn't bother to unwrap all the bandages to check his identity. Why would they? Who switches bodies in a hospital? According to his wishes, the body that they thought was Ambrose was cremated. Ambrose is safely in a sort of witness-protection, somewhere, at least that was the plan.

So, you are his replacement. That hasn't been announced publicly yet. I thought you were just here as a temporary consultant or advisor. Damn, I'm the reason my little brother is now in danger."

"Wait, wait, wait. Assuming I believe your story about Ambrose, what did he know that put him in danger? And more to the point, does it put me in the same position?"

"Lee, I honestly don't know. As they say, it's above my pay grade. I just took care of the details."

"Daniel, do you at least know who wanted him dead or who wanted him alive? More basically, I guess I want to know what sort of people my brother works for. If you can't answer that, at least just tell me this. Is my big brother one of the good guys or the bad guys?"

"If I were a better person, I might know the answer to that. I don't know if I can tell the good guys and bad guys apart these days. The best I can say is that I selfishly like to think I'm one of the good guys. I don't know what Ambrose found out, but odds are that it was connected to the Alien Encounters project since I was sent to snoop around and report on what was happening and, more pointedly, what was planned for the future."

"Yeah, about that. Rambo and Spook let me through the security system into the building to get my briefcase. How did you even get in here?"

"Strangely enough, the twins don't know it, but we three all worked together once upon a time. They kept upgrading their security systems at a certain location and I kept breaking through them. They should thank me;

challenging them like that made them as good as they are today. The security here is good but not the best. I can always work around just good.

Lee, I don't know about you, but I think that's enough of a family reunion for one night. Now that you know I'm alive and I know you might be in over your head here, I can assure you that we will meet again. In the meantime, for your own safety, this meeting never happened. I can trust you, can't I, little brother?"

"You can trust me, big brother…this time." I crossed the room to grab my briefcase but, when I turned to ask him when I might see him again, he was gone. As I walked to my car, I was surprised that this whole episode didn't leave me more disturbed. Maybe I was becoming numb to the unexpected. As Martha Stewart used to say, "it's a good thing."

[Personal Journal Entry #3

Objectively, I didn't have a good reason to trust Daniel, but he was my brother, and he didn't kill me so that was a good start, wasn't it? And if I decided to expose him, what would I even say, "I bumped into a guy lurking in the building last night but I don't think he had time to do any harm so I thought I would just wait until this morning to mention it." That would just get me in trouble instead of Daniel. I would probably lose my security clearance, then lose my job, I could never again go out to dinner with the twins, and I might even piss off the pope. Nope, nothing to tell. Nothing happened. Trust me.]

Chapter 8 – Same Problems, New Toys

The team was meeting in the large conference room this morning since there was too much "show and tell" stuff today to fit in the smaller secure room. I was still thinking more about Daniel than the good news / bad news briefing we had yesterday afternoon. I was worried about him; what he was involved in sounded dark and dangerous. I was also worried about myself now. Putting two and two together it struck me that there was probably a connection between Ambrose's non-accident and Steven's claim that Ambrose was anxious to make public what might be some very disturbing findings. However, considering the long list of players holding secrets, I couldn't really guess which secrets pushed whose panic button. I don't know what Daniel meant when he said we would meet again. Was he talking years or was he still lurking nearby? I wanted to discuss all this with Gus, but then I would have to reveal my supposedly dead brother's connection with what I collectively think of as "dark forces" and possibly expose Ambrose to more danger, if it turned out that he was alive. Well, actually, Daniel said "probably alive;" I'll try to think positively about that.

Today was all about getting familiar with the sophisticated equipment that we will use on site to gather every tiny bit of data connected with a UAP appearance. I've seen most of it in action watching the show last season and was amazed at the amount of information collected. I recognized the sensor array for just about any known type of radiation and the gadgets for night vision, as well for seeing infrared and ultraviolet. In the corner was a LIDAR [light detection and ranging] unit and the small lasers that went with it. The LIDAR was mostly used in determining distances but was also good at estimating the size of an anomaly. There were also another looking larger, more sinister laser.

That one looked like it could punch right through something relatively close or could blind a craft at even quite a distance – haven't seen anything like that on camera before. Beyond that lurked several impressive looking pieces of equipment that left me baffled. The science department back at the university would have killed to have some of this stuff.

Thomas "Tesla" Williams – our self-proclaimed "wizard of all things electronic" and "dark lord of the internet" – was leading today's meeting. My other team members tended to have a more professional demeanor, but I was comforted that at least one other member, besides me, had definite "geeky" inclinations. [*I wonder where he comes down on the Star Trek v. Star Wars debate?*] I think Tesla was more comfortable with gadgets than with people, but he was very good at his job. While no one said that we couldn't bring donuts and coffee into the meeting this morning, Tesla did threaten bodily harm to anyone who spilled something on his precious equipment. And, in the same vein, he began the meeting.

"First of all, and with the highest priority, I want to implore all of you not to drool over my new toys. Hauling this equipment all over the planet, is hard on my delicate babies so, in fact, with a few exceptions most of this is brand new this year. And before Steven goes into heart failure, 'No, I did not exceed my budget and I did not rob an electronics supply store.' I would like to claim that my wizard level powers allowed me to just conjure up everything we need but that would be just too much work. [*Yep. I can spot a guy who plays 'dungeons and dragons' at a hundred yards.*] Instead, I have arranged with the manufacturers of these goodies to highlight them on air and list them in the on-screen credits at the end of each episode. Win-win for everyone.

These upgrades give us top of the line, state-the-art sensor capacity. This season we will be able to detect our prey – sorry, I mean the UAP – faster, at greater distances and with more precision. However, as Steven told us, our goal this season is not just to look on passively and take notes. We want to engage a response from them and try to communicate with them, even if we aren't sure what they are saying back to us. So, this season we have an increased capacity to broadcast, to reach out and tap them on the shoulder as it were. [*I'm not sure the Grays have shoulders*] We can project various types radar, radio waves, and radiation at them up and down the light spectrum; we have a big powerful laser that will be hard to ignore and finally we have a very special focused broadcast system that we can concentrate to a field only about 3 feet wide at a distance of over half a mile.

That last remark clicked on something in my memory, but before I could pin it down Arthur interjected, "I read that the Army was testing something like that focused radar back in the late 1940's at the air base in Roswell. The author claimed that testing that radar was the cause of the famous crash in '47. Do you think that we might poking the bear a little too hard?"

"Arthur, I've read that same article and a few others that suggest that the increase in UAP crashes matches our increased use of commercial radar at airports or for weather prediction. In my opinion, the flaw in that argument is that we don't have any crashes at airports or military bases where radar is heavily in use. So, my thought is that if radar did affect UAP it had to be a be at a very limited frequency, not widely used, or just as our equipment has gotten better ET has upgraded their stuff too.

This isn't a secure briefing, but please don't repeat me on this. But after all the reports of UAP harassing our pilots, wouldn't it be fun knock of one of them out of the sky for a change?" [*It surprised me a bit, but there seemed to be general agreement with that sentiment from the team. Hmm, maybe the team is a little more "blood thirsty" than I had given them credit for. Works for me*.]

Now it was my turn to interrupt with a concern, "Let's say that prodding a UAP with some of Tesla's new toys does provoke a response. How much of a response are we looking for? I know our ultimate goal is communication but starting up communication can be very tricky."

At this point Spook – or it could have been Rambo since he wasn't in his "uniform" today – speaks up. [*And really neither of them ever talk much other than answer questions on security issues.*] 'I think Lee has a point here. Think about trying to pick someone up in a bar. If you aren't careful, you are just as likely to get a slap in the face as you are to start a flirty conversation. What we really want here is that flirty conversation because an alien slap in the face might involve phaser beams or photon torpedoes. And for all our fancy equipment and theories, this really just our first time in a bar and looking for our first date."

"Thanks for your rather colorful support. [*I don't use a name because I'm still not sure which twin spoke up.]* We can't plan ahead for everything, but what are we aiming for on our first outing? Do we want to just get them to notice us? Do we want them to somehow acknowledge our presence? Do we want to keep poking them until they make a significant response? Maybe take a half-hearted swat at us like we're an annoying insect? And what if they do "shoot a phaser" at us?" That produced some pretty thoughtful looks around the group, so I decided to forge ahead.

"Military folk often say that 'no plan survives contact with the enemy.' I'm not asserting that the UAP are the enemy. I just think we need to remember that all elaborate plans we come up with this week, could all just fall apart if we have an actual experience of contact. It's all different this season because we aren't just observing and recording. We are, to borrow Arthur's colorful phrase, 'poking the bear.' We don't know how subtle or how bizarre contact with that bear might be."

It's Shannon's turn to pipe up now. "I have to agree with Arthur, Lee and Spook [*Ok, it was Spook*]. This is all, pardon me for borrowing the Spook's scenario, "virgin territory" for us. I mentioned this yesterday and I have been thinking about this a lot. I think there might be an approach that's more than observing but a lot less than Telsa's laser canon". [Telsa growns a bit, 'I never get to have any fun.' A round of mock sympathetic 'Ah's' follow.]

Shannon forges ahead after the interruption, "I know this has come up before and was dropped because it didn't meet the 'hard science' approach that we try to follow. On the other hand, since we are trying new approaches this season, it might be the perfect time to set aside our prejudices and consider the psychic angle again. It's not hard data, but a lot of stories consistently insist that the Greys were able to get inside people's heads, that they were definitely telepathic. Maybe that is a sort of midway approach that they can respond to comfortably because it recognizes who they are and uses something familiar to them.

Back to Telsa, "I don't know guys, this psychic stuff just seems so 'out there,' so weird to me."

Back to Shannon. "Says the guy who is trying to talk to aliens."

And back to Tesla, "Ok, point taken. Let me approach this from a more practical angle. Would our audience really take something like that seriously? In fact, would any of you?"

This time Gus takes the floor in a tone that is serious but not offended. "I do. And so would a lot of the viewers. For centuries saints and mystics, Buddhist monks and Moslem holy men, have exhibited extraordinary mental abilities. Those abilities have been verified time and again by both believers and by unbiased observers. We have all this incredible equipment but if there is one more resource that we could tap, we would be foolish to ignore it just because just because its unfamiliar to us and out of our control."

Maybe he considers that an insult to his precious toys, but Tesla isn't quite ready to give in, "Let's say we decide to try this angle. Where do we find this psychic who is talented, verified, fairly normal and willing to work with us on such short notice? I'm pretty sure we can't just call up the local psychic hotline."

"I'm sure they are out there," says Gus, "but you're right that we don't have the time to do extensive interviews. There is a possibility though. I don't know her, but I have heard of a woman who might fit the profile you just gave. She lives in South America; I think it was Chili, but I could be wrong. When she was much younger, she occasionally helped her mother who was a cleaning lady in the trauma unit at a Children's Hospital. It didn't take long for staff to notice that some kids seemed to make a drastic improvement almost overnight. It did take them a while to connect that with her rounds with her mom.

When they seriously looked into what was happening, they found out that Isabella – Yeah, that was her name – could literally see the trauma that a child had experienced and then calmly walk them through it, soothing whatever fears that trauma has engendered. Since then, she has helped authorities find missing people, and people with amnesia quickly restore their memories. She says that using her power consistently leaves her weak. And as a result, she has become a bit of a recluse. She avoids large crowds and limits herself to using her gifts a few times a week for especially serious needs. The locals consider her to be a living saint."

Steven, ever the practical one, retakes the lead. "She does sound like a good candidate, but like you said, Gus, we don't know her and how would we ever persuade her to leave her home and look for aliens?"

"You know, I think I do know someone who has met her. And he can be incredibly persuasive. It's about lunchtime, so, with your approval, Steven, I could try to call him as soon as we break up. It might take a while to get through to him and even longer to see if he can make this happen, but it just might work and it is certainly better than the psychic hotline."

"Alright, Gus, give it a try. You have pulled off some against-the-odds stuff in the past and maybe your luck is still holding. Everyone else, lunch break. Be back here in 90 minutes. And then Tesla might let you play with some of his toys."

"Toys, he calls them. I get no respect for my ultra-high tech, absolutely indispensable contributions, to our work."

"You called them toys," snapped Shannon.

"Yeah, but they're my toys."

Everyone wanders off to lunch, except for Gus and me. I was being nosy, but I couldn't help myself. "Are you calling who I think you are calling?"

"And just who do you think I'm calling?" says Gus with that knowing smirk of his.

"I think you are calling the same person whose recommendation got me this job; you know, 'the big guy' in Rome."

With a flourish, Gus pulls out a very expensive looking phone and taps one button.

"Oh. My. God. You have the pope on speed dial?"

"Keep your voice down. And no, this is just his personal secretary. If "the big guy" isn't available, the secretary can pass on a message for me. And I'll call back later."

With a huge grin I admit, "this is just so awesome! I actually know a guy who has the pope on speed dial! I feel so humbled."

"You are such a fanboy," say Gus as he shoos me away and starts speaking in Italian.

[Personal Journal Entry #4

Someone else at my age and station in life might find Gus's "fanboy" comment a bit insulting. But I admit to myself that it is kind of true, at least in some cases. When it comes to the British Royal Family or to the Pope, I'm hooked. I think it's because I grew up in a dull little town, I spent most of my youth reading and studying so I could get a dull job as a science teacher. I've never fallen in love or even dated a pretty girl, I never risked new adventures. I would tell myself, I'm too tired or too busy or it's not the right time. The truth is my life is dull; I'm dull [insert heavy sigh]. When I see the color and pageantry, the rituals and customs surrounding royalty or the pope, it like a trip to fantasy land for me. It's all the things my life has been missing, and for some reason it just gives me a thrill to even look on at a distance.

Yeah, I hear it now. I just quit my job and left home to hunt aliens; I was attacked by my ninja dead brother, and I have a friend with the pope on speed dial. That's nowhere close to dull. Odds are I am finally feeling a little homesick and more than a bit overwhelmed by my new situation and all these amazingly talented people on the team. Still... I do think I belong here and can be a vital resource for the team – I know I do, and I can because I have repeated that mantra to myself about a thousand times in the last few days. Give me a few more days and the pond won't seem so big, and this little fish won't feel so small.

Then again, maybe it's Gus's fault. Hanging around an international man of mystery on a clandestine mission for the pope, that is bound to be a little intimidating for a small-town guy. He's probably chatting with pope right now. [And one last fanboy moment] He chats with the Pope – how awesome is that!!]

[Personal Journal Entry #5

This might be just a continuation of Entry #4 where I mention all the "amazingly talented people on the team." Our long lunches have given me a chance to get to know these people a lot better.

Steven George heads the team but I still don't have a clear image of him in my head. Other team members describe him as "serious, determined or workaholic." He always seems terribly busy; he doesn't share lunch with us or chat during breaks. I suspect that, much like me, he is an introvert who needs some quiet alone time to recharge his social batteries.

Arthur Doyal is the oldest team member, and he reminds me of a cross between Mr. Rogers and Sherlock Holmes. I even asked if his middle name was Conan – like the author of those Sherlock Holmes books, Sir Arthur Conan Doyal. He rather shyly admitted that it was. His mother had been a huge fan of the detective and she got her way when his name was chosen. Arthur spent most of his professional career as a historian with an interest in archeology. He said that it was only with his more recent investigations into "lost civilizations" that he started to consider the influence of "outsiders" on our development. That eventually lead him back to the 21st century and our current quest for UAP.

Thomas Williams, who will only answer to his nickname of Tesla, is the youngest of the team. When it comes to UAP or UFO's, he is a long time "true believer." On a cross country driving vacation when he was in middle school, his family took a long detour off their route to visit Roswell, NM. He says there was nothing to see at the crash site since the government had long ago scraped the area clean and hauled everything off to Wright Field in Dayton. But the town of Roswell was UFO heaven. The family took in all the exhibits; bought tons of souvenirs and he was hooked. He read all the UFO books and later, in high school, he and three friends camped out at the gate to Area 51 for three days hoping to see something otherworldly. They did see some odd lights in the sky, but his friends said it was just some of the prototype aircraft they tested there. But Tesla said he just knew in his heart that it was aliens encouraging him to keep looking.

Shannon Timmons worked part-time as an EMT through college and grad school. She has some stories both horrendous and hilarious about those days. I guess that sort of thing might tend to "toughen you up" as a person. During the show's off-season, she likes to get out her motorcycle and do long road trips with some friends. But I don't think that – or a leather jacket – is enough to earn her an official "bad girl" badge.

Even I used to ride my brother's old motorcycle, after he had gone off to the army and I finally got it to run. However, I didn't go on long trips; I stayed close to home where I was on familiar territory. I liked to ride alone; no one can bother you when you ride alone, it was a safe space for an introvert like me.

I still don't know much about Rambo or Spook. Instead of hanging out with the main team, they move around and try to get to know everyone on the crew. I suppose when your job is security that is what you need to do. I heard them use the term "situational awareness;" maybe there is some military connection in their still hidden background.]

Chapter 9 – First Contact – for this season anyway

We were all heading for the small conference room again this morning as I spotted Gus entering the building. I hung back a bit to talk with him more privately. "Gus, I didn't see you again after lunch yesterday. Did your call go well?"

"It did, but it took a lot longer than I had anticipated." In a slightly more hushed tone he adds, "When the big guy got my message, the secretary said he definitely wanted to talk with me, but he had an extremely busy schedule yesterday. It was, of course, evening in Italy when I called, and he was having a dinner meeting with some dignitaries who had been bumped out of their assigned appointment earlier in the day. All I could do was wait for him to finish up. A couple of hours went by till his secretary called and connected us. Long story, short, he agreed to help but can't make any guarantee. He was intending to make a personal phone call to Isabella the next day. I've heard him make "a personal appeal" to people before; I've never heard anyone tell him no.

I'll let Steven know that it is looking good, but working out all the details and figuring out how to accommodate any concerns Isabella might have could take a few weeks. She definitely won't be on board for the first excursion since that leaves next week. We'll have to let Tesla do the "poking" on that one."

The session began with Arthur giving us a detailed list of possible locations. The basic criteria were simple enough. We were looking for definite activity verified by multiple witnesses.

- There has to be a pattern of continuing appearances and the last appearance should be recent – no more than two weeks ago. We don't trek off to some God forsaken location that hasn't seen a UAP in 6 months. Odds need to favor that they will be back.

- The UAP can't just flash through the area but needs to stay put. Tesla says that ideally his instruments need at least 2 minutes to get good solid data. *[I was used to seeing the ticktack videos where they are there and then gone in a few seconds. I was surprised when Arthur mentioned that a lot of the best sightings lasted over 30 minutes.]*

- The sightings need to be someplace readily accessible. If there were claims that a saucer fleet was prepping for something in the Himalayan Mountains, we would reject that location because there is no way to get all our equipment out there.

I didn't expect that there would be a long list of locations that fit our requirements, but it took us the rest of the day to review the list and narrow it down to our final choice. In the end I was a bit disappointed. We obviously passed on war zones and countries that were not too fond of Americans. We skipped a couple of European countries that I have always wanted to visit because the supposed sites just seemed too "touristy." One location on an exotic pacific island appealed to me, but getting all our equipment there would entail a long boat trip and it would really mess with our schedule.

Our choice for our first attempt at "tapping on ET's shoulder" – which was now Arthur's favorite phrase, would be [*drum roll, please*] Luckenbach, Texas. Don't be surprised if you never heard of it; no one has. At the last census, it had three official residents. Luckenbach is really just the nearest name on the map to our final destination. We are ultimately headed to "Cattle Haven Ranch," a huge spread near Luckenbach owned by Rich and Lisa Donahue. Though most of the population on the ranch consists of cattle, [*as one might expect given* the name of the ranch] it was a large operation with lots of ranch hands [*Cow pokes? Cowboys? I not sure how they identify*]. Those workers have reported strange things in the sky for years, but the area has been especially active for the last four months with at least eight events witnessed by more than one person – and it wasn't on a Saturday night after a visit to the "Boozy Udder" [*that is so gross*] which, we have learned, is the nearest bar to the ranch. The bar is about the only thing near the ranch except for the one stop gas station-post office-grocery store-building supply and barber shop located in [*where else?]* Luckenbach. Rambo immediately decided to refer to the area by a very crude nickname which I can only say rhymes with "dumb luck." Gus would be missing from this first trip; he was somewhere in South America getting Isabella ready to join our crew. I'm not sure which location – Texas or S. America – was preferable; we'll have to compare notes when he returns.

On the positive side the area was easily accessible, roads were decent though unpaved, and our trucks would have no problem bringing in our equipment. The ranch owners, Rich and Lisa, were very welcoming and excited about what we were doing. They told us over some nice cold lemonade that there were a couple cases of cattle mutilation about a decade ago, but they seemed to lack the precision of other cases they had seen on TV – probably that rival show on the Discovery Channel. The sheriff was inclined to think it was just teenage pranksters trying to stir up trouble. He said after the Hanson brothers moved to Dallas, the mutilations ended. No cattle mutilation was just fine with us. We weren't doing cattle autopsies anyway, though Shannon would have been happy to oblige if one were needed. I think it was Rambo who joked that if Shannon got bored there would be no safe place for the cattle to hide.

And, of course, there was a negative side to this site – but only slightly negative it turned out.

The bunkhouse was full of cowpokes [*or cowboys or whatever*] and the nearest motel was about an hour and a half away from here. The producers decided that this was not a problem and arranged for tents and portable bathroom facilities and a mobile kitchen – I was later informed that the proper local terminology was "chuck wagon." [*I wonder what made Chuck so famous?*] Ironically, I found the thought of "camping out" in "the middle of nowhere," Texas, in the hot summer to be chilling. However, I have to admit that, in hindsight it wasn't so bad, and I learned a new term, "glamping." Each "tent" was a nice sized, air-conditioned space with electricity and even Wi-Fi. My tent was nicer than the apartment I had been living in back when I was broke. Granted an ensuite bathroom would have made it perfect but the facilities we had were clean, decent and close enough for late night convenience. There was one more Big Bonus! It turns out our meals were being catered and were a couple Michelin Stars above the studio's rubber chicken.

Early the next morning everyone got busy setting up the equipment site. We were about a mile from our tent city and just over a small rise. This was near where the most recent sighting had taken place and it has the advantage of there being very little light pollution from the main ranch facilities.

Telsa's toys were fun to look at back at the studio, but they were even more amazing as he explained their set up. He was very proud of he referred to as his "targeting system." All of the sensor arrays and scanners were hooked to a central computer that could use the data to triangulate the exact location of anything they detected. [*Goodbye binoculars*]. This location was then fed to motorized self-focusing, high definition, long range cameras. [*Wasn't that a mouthful.*] When we were still fine-tuning the setup, Tesla took a crystal-clear stop motion picture of a bird in flight that I couldn't even see with binoculars. No more of those fuzzy was-that-a-saucer-or-a-frisbee pictures. And the best was yet to come. He had just received a long-range video camera that was promised to be just as sharp. It would take a day or so to fully integrate it into the targeting system and recording devices.

After the hustle to get things ready, there came the hard part – waiting. Like many of our airlines, UAP don't follow a predictable schedule. The ranch people said one was due. They claimed the cattle felt it and were restless. Are cattle noted for being psychic or is that just a common animal thing? There are many reports that dogs are sensitive to UAP activities. If Gus can't get us that South American lady, maybe we should at least get a couple of dogs – with the bonus that they would be fun to play with on boring days when nothing was pinging our sensors.

As it turned out our timing was almost perfect. In the afternoon of the third day after our arrival, the equipment started to register "an anomaly." The targeting computer seemed to have picked out an empty spot in the sky as the source of the disturbance. At first the super cameras didn't see anything. Then, literally, in the blink of an eye, the sensors went wild and there it was. The cameras had it now and it was clearly a solid saucer shaped craft. It was hovering about 50 feet above the terrain. The computer estimated its diameter at about 45.55 feet across – which was almost disturbingly precise. We couldn't tell if it was revolving or not because the surface was smooth and uniform. It was hard to tell from looking at the monitors, but the computer notified us that it had a slight wobble at seemingly random intervals.

We had just recorded the most accurate hard data about a UAP to date. Since the craft's data hadn't changed much for about 5 minutes, we tore our eyes off the monitors and Tesla finally broke the silence to ask Steven, "what's our next step, boss."

Cautiously Steven replie, "what is the least aggressive sort of prodding that we could do right now?"

"The simplest would be a directed broadcast on varying radio frequencies, that repeat every15 seconds aimed right at them but not too intense. AND that happens to be the test package I had just programed into the system so it's ready to go immediately."

"Do it," Steven ordered and then continued more thoughtfully, "Do you have any guess how they might experience that on their end. What have we given them to react to?"

"Ah, there's the question. What's it like to be an alien?" After making sure the program was running properly, Tesla pondered Steven's question and said, "If it were aimed at us, it would register on our communication systems but wouldn't do any damage. Once the pattern started to repeat, we would know that it wasn't natural or accidental. I would at least want to know where it was coming from." A few seconds later the targeting system let out a squawk and told us the target was gone, not that it moved off in a certain direction, just gone.

It took about half an hour to synchronize the data for review.

Wow, I had just seen my first live UAP, and as the saying goes, "you never forget your first." On the first data run through we concentrated on the UAP's appearing and disappearing act. Most of the questions were directed to me as the theoretical physics guy. "Well, I'll have to it take very slowly and study the details to see if it confirms my suspicion or not. But if I can speculate, what we just saw seems to be an example of a craft traveling through a portal of some kind rather than through regular four-dimensional space-time. With a portal you can start here and end there, but you don't travel the distance in between. That is not something we can do or even explain very well but we do have some contemporary theories that would allow for that possibility."

"Lee, I've just coordinated the time stamps for the video and the radio broadcasts. You all need to see this." Whatever it is, Tesla looked like a kid finding a ton of Christmas presents under his tree.

"It's slight so I missed this the first time but watch what happens each time the broadcast starts to repeat." At the beginning of each broadcast, the saucer showed a distinct wobble. "They noticed us, the broadcast affected them, and then they left. That's what we were looking for, wasn't it? Get their attention and evoke a response. Granted we don't understand the response or why we caused it, but it happened. Now that we know our methods are working, we can try being a little more insistent next time and maybe get an even better response.

Let celebrate people, we done good today!" Tesla is very happy with his toys. Everyone, including me, is hyped up as we return to our tent city for the night.

After today's excitement, what would tomorrow bring? It didn't bring anything. For the next week the equipment was silent. The only good thing about the lull had been that we had a lot of time to review all the data - backwards, forwards, inside out; there was a lot of time on our hands. At the end of the week Steven decreed that we pack up and head home. Back at the studio we would take all that material and craft it into the first episode of the new season. Meanwhile we investigated our next research location and talked endlessly about "the next step."

[Personal Journal Entry # 6

For me personally the trip to Texas was a huge success. I found out that "glamping" could be fun and best of all I saw my first UAP. Sure, I had written about them but now, having really seen one, I felt more honest as a writer. Of course, as I tend to do, once I look at the bright side of something I can't resist turning it over to check out the dark side. There were unanswered questions even as we upped our game for the next round. How much of a response were we ready for? When did tapping become poking? How much could you "intensify" things before the aliens perceived our efforts as aggressive or hostile? We didn't know. I just hoped we don't figure it out it's too late.]

Chapter 10 – Highs and Lows

With the heart of a true bureaucrat, Steven insisted that our reports on "the incident" refer to that amazing experience as "Texas Encounter One" [*you can just feel that term sucking the excitement out of the event.*] In a mild act of rebellion, the team just referred to it as "T1" which sounded a bit more mysterious.

Let's pause for a little perspective. The tense, high energy, adrenaline rush of what the crew almost reverently referred to as "the incident" lasted, from first blip on a screen to the grand finale vanishing act at the end, for less than 10 minutes. Our entire "camping trip" in Texas lasted for slightly over 10 days. That left a lot of people with a lot of time on their hands.

Sure, we had plenty of data to scour and debate as we hoped for an encore performance from ET, but, at best, data mining was boring, and doing it under the hot Texas sun was hellishly boring. The only person having fun during that "week when nothing happened" was Shannon. She scoured the area, where the saucer had hovered, with an extremely fine-toothed comb. She didn't find a crop circle or mutant prairie dogs to dissect, but she managed to collect a couple crates of "suspicious specimens" for further study in her lab.

Reasonably, the primary team and our assistants couldn't leave the site lest ET catch us off guard but some of the auxiliary staff, technicians and set up crew were chomping at the bit to track down that fabled bar in Luckenbach. I never saw the place but those who frequented it that week said that with some remodeling and a few upgrades it just might reach the status of a dive. But the place did have cold beer, a pool table, and a juke box, and in "dumb luck" Texas that was as close as you would ever come to Club Med.

A couple times guys did come back to tent city high on cheap booze but, let's face it, a hangover under the hot Texas sun definitely qualified as one of the circles of Hell. [*Had Dante lived in Texas I'm sure he would have included it.*] Most of the crew was on their good behavior because they didn't want to lose access to the one oasis to be found within a two-hour drive. In fact, the bar owner, a rangy looking old timer who went by "Buck," drove out to thank Steven because in that one week he had almost doubled his normal income for the month.

When we got back from Texas everyone took a long weekend to unwind. I wouldn't have missed "T1" for the world. I got to experience my first "close encounter" of some kind and, despite my initial dread – I had never gone camping as a kid, tent city wasn't so bad. [*Yes, an air-conditioned tent may not count as "camping" for some people, but it was a brave new world for me*] However, I was looking forward to my "scorpion free" apartment and sleeping in my own comfy bed.

I had picked up a pizza on my way home and was looking forward to a quiet evening just vegging out in front of the TV. I came in, set the pizza on the kitchen island, and grabbed a beer out of the refrigerator. I decided to change clothes first and get comfy in some old sweats before I settled in for the evening. I left my feast on the counter and headed for my bedroom.

As soon as I stepped inside, a hand on my mouth and an arm around my throat. "Keep quiet and I'll let you loose," said a now familiar voice. ["*Not again," I thought*.] And as a protest I bit his hand – he was foolishly not wearing a glove this time.

"Ow, what's wrong with you? You bit me, little brother."

Now I really did want to scream, "What's wrong with me? What's wrong with you? Why couldn't you just knock on my door and say 'Hi' like a normal person?"

"Well, that wouldn't be any fun and I'm not your average normal person.

"Fun, he says," I mumble. "Go grab some pizza off the counter, I'll change clothes and be right out."

I came out of the bedroom to find Daniel on the coach, munching pizza and drinking MY BEER. "You took my beer." I said flatly.

"You have more in the frig," he grinned. [*Brothers! Did I really miss this?*]

"How do you know I have more beer? Did you search my apartment?"

"Of course, I did. I had some time to kill, and you will be happy to know that your apartment is bug free and secure."

"Secure? Why wouldn't it be secure? Daniel, talk!"

"Ok, so I was talking with one of your crew at the "Boozy Udder" one night…"

"You were in Texas???"

"So were you. Now, eat your pizza and let me go ahead with my story. Well, I may have added a little "booster" to one of his drinks and he happily described everything that had happened out on the ranch. I reported most of it to my superiors and they were VERY interested and instructed me to keep a closer watch on your team.

Lee, you have to know that the more you uncover, the more you will be in danger. I've thought about it and have decided that I have to go back to "plan A" where I join your auxiliary staff and I can keep an eye on you. Sometime tomorrow morning, Steven will find out that he has lost one of his set-up crew and magically I will be on the top of his list of possible replacements.

"Lost?" It wasn't quite a shout; let's call it an intense question. "You didn't kill him, did you? Please, tell me you didn't kill someone so you could babysit me."

"I didn't kill anyone... I didn't have to this time. [*I'm not sure that was as comforting as Daniel might have intended*.] It seems my chatty friend from the bar had an ex-wife and six kids for whom he has not been paying court-ordered child support. He had ditched his family two states away and was comfortable that the "she-monster" wouldn't track him down. Unfortunately for him, his "ex" got an anonymous tipoff that he was working for the studio under a fake ID. After she called him – strangely that "tip" also included his phone number - He faced the choice of being arrested or going on the run again. He turned in his resignation, collected his pay and left town this afternoon.

"Didn't you ditch 'plan A' because I would recognize you? That hasn't changed."

"That's true, but now you already know that I'm not dead, so you shouldn't be surprised to see me and accidentally give away my cover. I have thought this through very carefully so here's how this is going to go so you won't have to act awkward around me. A couple of days after I start working at the studio, I'll come over to talk to you in the cafeteria. I'll say I just heard that you are secretly the writer, Andy Leland, one of my favorite authors. I'll say I just wanted to say 'hi' but, if you ever had some free time, I would love to discuss a couple of your articles. Now it's public knowledge that we know each other and if I sometimes talk with you, I'll just be a fan with questions about your work, rather a creepy stranger who is stalking you. Perfect, huh?"

First Gus and now Daniel. How many more people will I have to pretend to be strangers? "When I meet you "for the first time" in the cafeteria, who will you be? "

"I will still be Daniel. You might slip up if I used a new name. However, I won't be Daniel Andrews. That would just be too much of a coincidence. I'll be Daniel Jordan."

Aw, he had picked mom's maiden name. That gesture touched a soft spot in my heart - as I'm sure he already calculated it would. It sounded like a crazy sitcom plot when Daniel laid out his plan, but it could work. [*Also, I probably couldn't get rid of him if I tried. A dog with a bone would be less determined.*] There might be one snag though, so I ask, "Have you even read anything I've written?" And I was surprised again.

"I've read almost everything you have written, except for your pretentious physics professor stuff. [*Pretentious, I'm not pretentious. That's just how scholars write.*] You are good at talking about obscure things in an easy-going way for us non-intellectual peasants, and you're even funny sometimes." [*Not the answer I expected – and yep…there was that soft spot again*]

After we finished our pizza and beers, I got Daniel to promise that he would stop lurking in the dark and ambushing me. As a gesture of good faith, I even gave him a key to my apartment. We talked about a lot of random things that evening. There were obviously dark corners in his life that were off limits, yet I felt comfortable that this ninja-cat burglar-super spy was still basically my reckless, cocky brother and it was nice to have him back.

I took the empty pizza box and beer bottles to the kitchen and returned to ask where Daniel was staying. He was gone. That vanishing act of his is just creepy; it's like an alien stepping through a portal. I have to convince him to stop doing that.

[Personal Journal Entry #7

I was still annoyed about getting mugged in my own bedroom, so I didn't tell Daniel that having him around does make me feel a lot safer. I have been alone for a long time now and it's nice to have some family again. Besides, that creep who neglected his wife and kids deserves to have his own life shaken up. Still…there is that nagging part of my brain that whispers "I hope he's telling me the truth and didn't just kill the guy and hide the body." I have got to stop flipping over rocks looking for the dark side. There's enough to worry about in the light of day.]

Chapter 11 – Heigh ho, heigh ho, it's off to work we go.

We start off the workday, following our long weekend, with a general staff meeting so Steven can give us our "marching orders" – his term, not ours. His first announcement was that our 10-minute incident in Texas had given us enough material for **three** episodes of Alien Encounters. The final production side of the show is new to me but as Steven spelled out his reasoning, it did make sense.

The first episode would focus on the capabilities of all our new equipment and then wow the audience with the speed with which we located the anomaly; then we would reveal the incredibly precise measurements we obtained, and finally knock it out of the park with the crystal-clear video of the saucer. In theory, the main team works in happy harmony on each episode, but in practice this first episode would be mostly Tesla's to assemble.

On the second episode we would all contribute as we talked about our efforts to get a response out of the saucer. Then would follow the amazing video of the saucer apparently reacting to the repeated broadcasts we aimed at them and then we finish with a discussion of what that reaction might mean in itself, and for future encounters.

The video highlights of the third episode would be the saucer just appearing out of nowhere and disappearing the same way. This episode would be mostly my baby. It was agreed that I would be the best one to try to explain inter-dimensional portals to an audience who often had trouble figuring out how to work their own smart phones. "Just keep it light," Steven instructed, "and don't mention things like an Einstein-Rosen Bridge. You'll be great!" As luck would have it, I had written an article on portals about a year ago, and I wouldn't have to "dumb it down" that much for the show. [*I hope that doesn't say something about the quality of the original article*.]

The second item on Steven's agenda was Gus's mission to South America. Isabella had agreed to work with us, and she and Gus would be arriving here in about a week to 10 days. There were some ground rules that Gus sent along for us to mind when Isabella arrived.

- Isabella can be uncomfortable with crowds, especially new people, so we shouldn't mob her or gang up on her when she first arrives.

- She says she will need some time to slowly move around and meet the team and all the crew individually. Gus explained that it's hard to find terminology for what she does but it's something like this. "An unfamiliar spirit" or stranger can upset Isabella's focus. Their presence is like static, and a lot of static can be unbearable. When she was a child, she could barely tolerate more than a few family members to be near her. As she grew older, though, she discovered ways to deal with that. Now it only takes her only a few moments to "read the texture" or characteristics of someone new to her. After that it isn't like she can ignore that person, but she can "allow herself to be at peace' with a known spirit. The important thing to remember is that she won't be reading our minds to uncover our deep dark secrets. She just needs to "recognize your spirit" so she will feel free to focus on any phenomena we encounter. There is something she can do, that she refers to the "merging of spirits," when, for example, she tries to help heal a traumatized child. However, that is deeper and more time consuming and only works with the person's free consent."

- The last phone call with Gus also disclosed something unexpected but possibly game changing. "When I first met Isabella, she barely spoke a half dozen words of English, but when she arrives you will notice that she is quite fluent now. It was a surprise for her too. She isn't sure if this is a new ability, or something that she just hadn't needed before now since she rarely leaves her hometown and had always been around Spanish speakers before I arrived. She says she was hardly aware of the change until I pointed it out. It's as though just having prolonged contact with me automatically gave her the ability to communicate with me. This could be significant because if she does manage to reach out to an alien mind, that talent might be an invaluable first step in opening a dialogue with them."

With that good news about Isabella, Steven turned to the last item on the agenda for today - choosing our next location for research. "We have narrowed it down to three that seem to have a lot of potential. All the details about each site are posted on our in-house web page. If you have anything to add that would make one stand out or maybe lose out, send me an email by the close of business tomorrow."

Two days later, we had our lottery winner. The crew started packing up our gear and each member of the main team hurried to put the finishing touches on those first three episodes. I almost felt like I was cheating because I already had that article on portals ready to go. *[I said "almost." I was now at this and appreciated any help I could find.]* Later that day, at lunch in the cafeteria, I found out that the newly hired member of our set-up crew was a big fan of Andy Leland's work. He seemed like a nice enough fellow, Daniel something.

Oh, and the lottery winner is a site near the city of Koumra, in the nation of Chad in Central Africa. I could be wrong, but I have an uneasy feeling that our accommodations there might not live up to the standards of "glamping" in Texas – and in case you are still wondering, "glamping" is a contraction for "glamour camping." I wonder if there is a word for what we are heading to in Africa.

[Personal Journal Entry # 8

I'm exhausted. The team has been trying to get the finishing touches on our assigned episodes that resulted from the Texas trip. The workdays were at least 12 hours long and on top of that we were getting ready to head to Africa. Africa! I never imagined going to Africa and my mind still brings up images of Tarzan swinging through the jungle. I did some research on Chad, so I was better prepared for this trip. No Tarzan; no Jane; but there were assorted monkeys around. Of course, we won't be staying in Koumra itself, which seems like a decent little city. We will be setting up shop about 45 minutes away because Aliens never appear anywhere near a decent Holiday Inn.

I heard from Gus today; it's taking a little longer than he had anticipated to accommodate Isabella's needs for traveling, so they now plan to join us in Africa instead of coming here to the studio first.

While I might be a whiz at quantum mechanics, I have never been good at languages. I am fluent in English, clumsy in Spanish, and that's it. This will be the first time in my life that I will be living in a place where I can't communicate with the local people. I wonder if aliens feel that way about coming here.]

Chapter 12 – "Rain drops keep falling on my head"

The word for our accommodations in Chad should probably be "mut" – which is unfortunately a contraction for mud hut. The producers claimed they found a great deal with a Safari company that leads tours through a nearby national park. Since it was "off season" they were willing to rent us all the "dwellings" where the tourists stayed to get that "authentic African Experience." The producers should have paid more attention to the words "off season" because no one in their right mind would stay in these "quaint, historic shelters" during the "high heat." The "muts" were definitely not air conditioned but, if there was a breeze, they might cool down to "simmer" rather than "roast." The other hint that this had not been the wisest choice was that none of our locally hired help lived in "muts." Apparently, they all lived in fairly nice houses in nearby

Koumra. [*And in fairness, I must admit that Koumra was a virtual Metropolis compared to Luckenbach.*]

The official languages of Chad are French and Modern Arabic. One of the crew knew a little Arabic, but not the local dialect; some of us had survived high school French but now wouldn't even try to order dinner in a French restaurant. In this regard the producers were on the ball. They had pre-arrange for three local Chadians [yes, that is the proper term] to join us as translators. After we had been on site for about 5 days, one of the translators, named Abakar, suggested that we make sure our electronic equipment was inside and off the ground because "the rains" were coming. Most of Africa only has two seasons, dry and rainy. Abakar says that in the days of his great-grandparents, the rains dependably came somewhere around late summer and lasted about 4 weeks. But now the rains were unpredictable and so rare that most of Africa was drought ridden. He was, however, certain that the rains would be upon us very soon. Shannan asked if he had read signs or omens in nature that pointed to rain. After he stopped laughing, he said, "No, miss, I have been checking out the satellite weather channel." Then the rest of us laughed and felt rather embarrassed that, for all our high-tech pretentions, we hadn't bothered to check that ourselves.

"The rains" did come during the night and, like an annoying relative, seemingly planned to hang around for a while. The music group Toto had a hit song [appropriately named "Africa"] that contained the line, "we bless the rains down in Africa." Unquestionably, the rain was a much-needed blessing, but to call what fell from the sky "rain" was like saying "Cattle Haven" ranch had a few cows, the Antarctic was a bit chilly, or that Bill Gates was well off. Looking outside was like staring into a waterfall. My immediate fear was that our mud huts would be washed away. When I voiced that concern, our translators had another laugh fest. It seems the tour company had more foresight than I had credited them. Our "mud huts" were, in fact, made of nice study concrete that had been made to look "mud-like" for the not very observant tourists [*and likewise not very observant scientists*].

On day two of the deluge, we tromped through rain and mud for our usual morning meeting with Steven. With our equipment hidden away from the rain, there wasn't much to report on or plan. Most of the team religiously followed the weather channel now but Steven still felt compelled to state the spirit dampening [*pun intended*] prediction that conditions varying from light rain to the occasionally heavy downpour would be with us for at least the next week.

The next day the rain was noticeably less intense and had periods when it was little more than a heavy mist, but the rain did indeed last for another eight days. That was unbearably long for us, but not nearly enough for this parched land. The real bonus was that the rain cooled things off, at least compared to the triple digit temps we had endured when we arrived.

Although Chad is a heavily Moslem country, the sale of alcohol is legal here and a couple of our intrepid crew quickly located a friendly liquor store in Koumra. Steven, as required by his position, warned everyone to stay sensible about their beverages of choice but he did allow us to turn one of the "muts" into a makeshift bar which we appropriately christened as "The Ark." Personally, I'm happy with the occasional beer, but even I looked forward the nightly "happy hour" to break the waterlogged monotony. Much to our surprise, Arthur was revealed to be a talented bartender who had worked his way through grad school mixing drinks at what he called "a high-end gentleman's club." [*Which we all knew was code for "strip club" but Arthur would neither confirm nor deny that.*]

Gus, Isabella and her companion, Maria Jose, had arrived in Chad just as the downpours started. With her crowd aversion, I wondered aloud how she tolerated busy airports and the close packed interior of a commercial jet. Steven assured me that they left from a small airport and traveled by private jet. Without thinking, I blurted out, "Where did we get a private jet?" Looking embarrassed and hesitant to answer, Steven quietly admitted that it was his. [*Bombshell alert*] The rest of the team knew his secret but had never got around to letting me in on it. There was an online, multiplayer fantasy game called [*How did I miss this?*] "Alien Encounters." I had even played it a couple of times; it was huge with gamers around the planet. Turns out that Steven had written it. He made a fortune from it and then turned his attention to his true love, actual alien encounters. That led to the TV show for which we all worked. I later pulled a couple of the team aside and inquired if there were any other secrets I should know before I stumbled into more embarrassing questions. They said there weren't. I want to believe them.

Between nasty weather and a few washed out roads it took three days for Gus and Isabella to make it to our site after they landed at N'Djamena International Airport – the only international airport in Chad. Isabella's family had insisted that it would be improper for her to travel alone with Gus – normally they would consider him "safe" since he was there as an envoy from the Vatican, but in their culture appearances mattered. Maria Jose was a widow, a cousin, and good friend of Isabella, so she had been asked – more likely ordered - by the family matriarch to join them. Gus privately told the team that even he had considered "grandma" to be scary and had been warned not to upset her or she would "put the evil eye on him." Though not at all superstitious, Gus also admitted that if anyone could put a curse on you, it would be Isabella's abuela.

Normally, i.e., when stepping outside wasn't like walking into a cataract, there would be large canopies all over our site where we would set up our equipment and find some shade, and we had one very large one that would double as cafeteria and meeting area. They too were temporarily stored away during the worst of the rain. Some of our muts were larger than others, with the largest of them being given over to "The Ark." This situation necessarily kept groupings of people on site to 7 or 8 – or maybe 10 if they were really close friends. And this limitation turned out to be the perfect setting for Isabella to meet and get to know the staff and crew.

Once she had settled in, Gus brought Isabella to meet the main team gathered in Steven's mut. After Gus briefly introduced each of us - Steven, Thomas [Tesla], Shannon, Arthur and me – he gave her a brief description of our specialties on the team. She then approached each of us in turn following this same routine with each person. She would take our hand, say our name and again introduce herself. ["*insert name*, I'm Isabella and I am happy to meet you."] Gus was right; her English was very good with only a trace of an accent. I had the feeling that Shannon would love to dissect her brain looking for what gave her this magical language learning ability. She wouldn't find anything; you could just feel that there was something deeply spiritual and very special about Isabella that would never show up under a microscope. [*Being the science guy of the group, that sentiment didn't sound very "Mr. Spock" of me but a good scientist wouldn't dismiss the data of his own experience – and what an experience this was.*] She spent about two hours with us, discussing what we hoped to achieve here and how she might help. She then asked to be excused to rest a bit and as she was leaving asked us to call her "Izzy" like her family did back home.

Once Gus and "Izzy" had gone, everyone was strangely quiet. It felt odd for our usually very vocal little group. After about a minute, I couldn't take it anymore and had to ask. "Ok, I have to know. Was that just me or did you feel something when she touched you?" The answers from around the team were each a bit different and yet eerily similar.

"I felt calm."

"At peace."

"I somehow felt that, in that moment, all was right with the world."

"I felt light, free. How did it feel to you, Lee?"

"I think I felt…safe."

You might have thought we would take some time to discuss what happened, but we didn't. It still felt special and fragile and – dare I say – sacred. In the days to come we did discuss this – a lot. We were still rain-bound for a few more days and each day Izzy would have a similar meeting with one, maybe two small groups, and each day we would hear quiet reports of each gathering ending with the participants not quite sure what they had experienced except that it was pleasant and refreshing. By the time the skies cleared, and we were getting our equipment set up again [post rain delay] it was obvious that everyone was now, to quote Rambo, "firmly on team Izzy."

[Speaking of Rambo, I would be amiss if I didn't relate what happened when Izzy came to meet his little group. Right after the main team, he was in the next group that she visited. Since she was staying secluded until the meeting process was complete and she was "at peace" with everyone, very few people had actually seen her yet. Rambo had seen Maria Jose picking up dinner from the kitchen and heard the gossip that she and Isabella were cousins. He must have assumed that the two women were about the same age. He, Spook and the new guy, Daniel, were betting on what Isabella would look like. Was she older or younger than Maria Jose? Rambo had just bet that she was old, gray haired and wrinkled. He was so wrong. When Gus and Izzy walked in to greet their little group, Rambo gasped to his brother, "Oh my God, she is so hot!" Spook told him to hush; Daniel said it was too late now because she could probably read his dirty mind anyway. Rambo turned red as a fire truck. And the story gets better, when the two of them were officially introduced she shook his hand, but she changed her usual greeting to, "Hello Peter, I'm Izzy and don't worry, I appreciate your approval." When she walked away, Rambo was still frozen in place like a bright red popsicle, still holding out his hand. And Spook and Daniel were doubled over laughing.]

[Personal Journal Entry # 9

My family was Catholic, and I considered myself to be a religious person, but I wasn't ready for the sort of spiritual experience that I got meeting Izzy. It was like she touched my soul and without a word let me know that everything would be ok, that I wasn't alone. I don't remember every feeling like that before. I think I had felt alone most of my life but had never recognized that until now.

Meeting Izzy seemed to be a unique and special experience for even the few hardened non-believers on the crew. I think there was comfort in knowing that there was more to this world than the cold march of cause and effect. I knew that unusual things happened at the quantum level; I liked knowing that they could happen in my everyday life too.]

Chapter 13 – Who says you can't learn anything useful from the movies?

After satellite radar confirmed that the rains had moved on, I was amazed how fast the crew got the open-air tents set up for our equipment, for the cafeteria, and just for places to get out of the hot sun. Everything was positioned just close enough to give the camp a "controllable security footprint" – to quote Rambo – and yet just far enough apart to allow any breeze to flow through.

Based on the sightings reported by the local population, we were in the right area. Though the interval between sightings varied and seemed random, appearances had been happening about every 7-8 weeks and it had been 9 weeks since the last one. Who knows, maybe the aliens also had a rain delay. We had no idea how portals might work but it did seem reasonable that opening one when the ski was filled with rain and perhaps lightning might be a problem. Their timing was definitely not under our control.

How we attempted to elicit a response was something we could control. Last time we hit them with a series of randomly chosen signals, because that was a sample program that Tesla had set up for a trial run and it was ready to go at the touch of a button. It seemed to do something. It was my suggestion that if they appear at this location [before we give up and go home] maybe we would seem more worthy of notice if the signal was clearly something constructed on purpose. This touched off a lot of debate about what would be a good introduction to humanity. No one believed that that the aliens were oblivious to our existence, but so far, our existence hadn't seemed to have had an impact on whatever they were up to.

Eventually we opened the discussion up to all the staff for suggestions since nothing was screaming "Pick me" to the team. Input ranged from the purely mathematical Fibonacci sequence to a recording of the word 'hello' in several languages. Whatever we finally chose, we wanted to be able to repeat it but with variations if the first attempts didn't seem to be working. The Fibonacci sequence wasn't really variable [or it wouldn't be a sequence]. We also worried about what the friendly - to us – 'hello' sounds might translate to in alien. [*Do you know what "cookie" sounds like in Hungarian? It's not good. What might "hello" sound like in Alien*?]

Someone from the staff – probably the cute blonde girl who always has earbuds in - suggested using a short piece of music. We liked that idea but "what sort of music" ended up being another round of debates. Halfway in jest, I eventually commented that "that series of four tones" worked well in the movie, Close Encounters of the Third Kind. Why don't we just use that? With uncanny speed people started humming that stupid earworm that would be forever stuck in our heads. In the end, without a criterion for something better, that became our new "tap on the shoulder." [*I'm picturing aliens humming those four tones and finding them just as annoying as we do. It could be a bonding moment.*]

The next day at about four in the afternoon, the computer started chirping and the targeting system aimed itself at a spot in the sky. This transit point was a bit closer to us than the one in Texas had been, and, like Texas, a saucer just appeared. The computer quickly confirms for us that the diameter matches exactly with the saucer in Texas but there was no way to tell if it was the same one or not. Scanners were collecting data and the cameras were all on target but nothing - that we could immediately see – seemed to be happening. After a couple minutes, Steven instructed Tesla to start broadcasting the tones and the response was immediate. After each set of tones there was a faintly detectible wobble to the craft. We had seen that same thing in Texas so we had predetermined that we would try something extra this time. "I'm going to start to vary the tones and slowly increasing the strength of the focused broadcast," came from Tesla. Again, there was a very gratifying response. The wobble happened when each set of tones finished no matter how fast or how slowly they were played.

While that was happening, Gus had escorted Izzy into the control center. Izzy goes from wide eyed wonder at what she is seeing on the monitors to a relaxed posture with her eyes closed to distraction. Almost instinctively the control center personnel go quiet so as not to disturb her concentration. It might have felt like a prayer meeting if it hadn't been for the hum and beeps of all the electronic equipment. Whenever the tone sequence varied and the saucer wobble would match. It was hard to tell on the monitors, but when we later reviewed the recordings more precisely, it looked like each increase in the strength of our signal produced a bit more wobble in the saucer.

About three minutes after Izzy arrived in the control center, she began to speak softly. One of the techs handed Gus a microphone to hold so whatever she said could also be recorded for later study. "I sense spirits, minds. There is more than one. They are not like any I have touched before."

Gus quietly asks, "Can you get any hint of what they are thinking or feeling?

"They are... strong minds. When I deal with human spirits, I have to explore, reach out to them. These minds broadcast, I feel them easily.

Sensing thoughts will be difficult. They are so different. I... I don't sense any feelings from them right now.

Humans have deeper and hidden levels that I can sometimes search through, here I see no depth. All is surface. All seem to have the same focus right now. There is exchange...maybe questioning. They are becoming more aligned, more of one mind."

"Do they sense you?" Steven asks.

"Compared to them my light is weak; but if they were closer or looking for me, perhaps they would.

There is a shift now… a decision maybe.

Now there is nothing."

All eyes were on Izzy until Tesla shouted, "They just disappeared again."

Immediately the staff came to life, checking data, comparing notes. It will take some time not only to process that data but to process what we had just heard from Izzy. She looked exhausted, but Maria Jose was at her side and helping her back to her quarters to recover.

Steven resolutely takes charge, "Let's keep a few techs on the system "just in case" but I doubt they will be right back. I want the main team to meet with me in my quarters in 15 minutes to share our immediate impressions and we all will reconvene at 9:00 AM tomorrow to do a detailed analysis of all the hard data. Lots to do; let's get busy."

Compared to the silence when Izzy spoke, the control center now buzzed with excited voices all talking at once. The team hung around for a few minutes in case there was something that needed attention immediately. Once we were comfortable that there was nothing earthshaking to note, the team headed out to gather in Steven's quarters. Shannon started off the discussion, "There are a couple of thoughts that I got from Izzy's interaction with the saucer. She did confirm some things that we had suspected.

First, there are definitely living beings in the saucer and that one was no surprise.

Second, it seems clear to me that they are telepathic and that is their usual way to communicate with each other; that had been the rumor but now we know for sure.

Third, I got a feeling that the longer Izzy was in contact with them, she seemed to be clearer about what she was experiencing. I think that is the same talent as her unusual ability to absorb the language of those with her and that might be the most important thing we learned today."

We agreed that Shannon's summary seemed to cover what we heard from Izzy. The rest of the hard data wouldn't be ready till tomorrow, but Arther noted that the general outline of our actions and their apparent response was very similar to our Texas experience – they appear, we poke, they react and then leave. Before we went off to a later than usual "happy hour" I wanted to share one more idea or maybe more of a question with the team. It might just be me looking at the dark side, but a few questions haunted me.

"I don't have a solid grasp on how all this telepathy works other than theories that it operates at the quantum level, but I wonder what happens if further contact does establish a better link between the aliens and Izzy. Does that make them more likely to detect her presence? I wonder if powerful telepaths, as they appear to be, might normally perceive weaker human minds as sort of a blank slate. It's not unheard of, but it is rare, to find a strong psychic talent like Izzy's among us, but that might be something they don't expect. I could be projecting my own impressions here, but Izzy seemed to sense them as orderly, maybe unemotional. How would such a being deal with the unexpected? How would we react say, to a stray dog that started talking to us?"

No one had an answer for that. Steven just told us to "chew on it" for later discussion. Tesla was anxious to get back to his toys and would likely be up long into the night reviewing that data. Shannon, Arthur, and I headed to "the Ark" where, by mutual but unspoken agreement, we talked about anything other than aliens. Clearly, this encounter had been much more significant than "T1" – it was longer, the response from the saucer was more evident, and Izzy input was revolutionary. I felt that it was too soon to pick it apart until we got all the details tomorrow and I think the others were in a similar mood.

[Personal Journal Entry # 10

I love trying to puzzle out the mysteries of hard science, but today's encounter made me very uncomfortable. Each piece of information we gained just confronted us with how much more we didn't know, and maybe even the dread of how much we don't even know that we don't know. We confirmed a direct connection between our broadcasts and the motion of the saucer – great! But did the aliens know it was us, or know that it was meant to be harmless? Did they even notice that it was happening or was it the saucer itself responding automatically to some outside interference?

We confirmed that the aliens are primarily, perhaps exclusively, telepathic – fantastic breakthrough! But how do we talk with someone who may not exactly have a language? How do they react to what they consider mute animals, if Izzy can share a thought with them? Will they want to protect that as treasure or eliminate it as a travesty?

In physics an answer often leads to more questions and hopefully more answers. The new answers can be challenging, or dazzling or unexpected, but they are never deadly. What happened today was amazing, but I keep turning it over to stare at the dark side. Have I always been this pessimistic or am I just discovering that I am still a timid little boy cowering from the shadows. It's not fair that Daniel can be so fearless, and I can't escape my fears.

Wow, all this self-reflection is depressing. I'm so glad I didn't start a diary when I was younger, it would have ruined my childhood. After an argument with a teacher [and I still maintain that I was in the right] a school counselor told me that I didn't like not having control of a situation; I thought he was crazy. Maybe I need to go back and apologize to Mr. Arlotta for doubting him.]

Chapter 14 – Tesla steals the show.

S ince this encounter lasted longer than the one in Texas and we were better prepared as to what to look for, there was a lot of data to sift through. Accordingly, the general review meeting was postponed from 9:00 AM until 1:00 PM just after lunch. To save Izzy from having to sit through a lot of high-tech stuff that most of us love to chew on, Steven asked her to summarize her experience first.

"I sensed minds unlike any I have faced before. It felt that communicating mind to mind was the normal practice for them. They didn't seem friendly and didn't seem hostile, they mostly seemed just "occupied" with some task. Tesla asked me later if I sensed that they were occupied reacting to our signals. I don't know their language, or if they even have one. At this point it was more like seeing images very briefly flashed across a screen. I didn't sense an image that might point toward our camp or activities, but much was exchanged among them, and it felt like I only sensed thoughts that they had in common - perhaps those are stronger, easier for me to receive.

As I told you, first meetings are physically exhausting for me and often unclear. I have found that later meetings are less tiring, and my impressions become clearer each time, perhaps that will be true of these visitors."

"Thank you, Isabella," Steven says. "You have provided us with information we never had access to before you agreed to join us. You're welcome to stay, or not, and listen to what else we learned, and, any time you want, feel free to take a break from the jargon and terminology that all these science geeks love.

Tesla has practically been bouncing off his seat, anxious to share what he has found, so the floor is his."

"Before I show you the good stuff, I want to mention something that occurred to me based on Izzy's experience and something that Lee had mentioned. It might be the case that the aliens are not actually aware of or reacting to our signals as we had supposed. The reaction, the wobble that we see, is rather small compared to the size of the craft. It might even be something that would routinely go unnoticed by them. I'm just suggesting that our broadcast may have interacted with some system on that craft but that it was not significant enough for that system to alert the crew. That hypothesis is less exciting than the notion that we had them dancing to our tune, but it is a real possibility.

However, I do have some exciting findings that we discovered later last night when sorting through input from various cameras. I'll start with two fascinating videos that we almost overlooked. After the main camera was locked on to the saucer, we then aimed one camera on the area beneath the saucer and one camera on the space above, just skimming the top of the saucer. We are assuming that since the craft is just hanging there, they must be using some kind of anti-gravity system.

Watch this view of a bird crossing from right to left on this monitor. It is gliding and not actively flapping its wings. It will pass over the saucer, starting at about 20 feet above it. By the time it has glided to the other side, it is 15 feet higher. There are two likely possibilities for what we are looking at. Either the pull of gravity above the saucer is less than outside its boundaries or the saucer is causing the air to rise around and over it and is pushing the bird higher. It could be both. However, it is clear proof that the saucer is obviously affecting the environment.

Now take a look at the area below the saucer. With the monsoon rains we have had, the ground there is covered with large, shallow puddles of water. When I zoom in a bit you can see that the water is rippling at a steady pace of every 1.8 seconds. And 7 seconds before the saucer vanishes the frequency of the ripples starts increasing rapidly. I don't know what all this means, I'm the electronics guy, but it's things we have never seen before. Lee, you're the physicist here. Does this mean anything to you?"

"Well, the bird confirms that the anti-grav effects extend beyond the saucer itself. It will take a while to research those vibrations, but the frequency might give us a hint to how this works. We haven't cracked the secret of an anti-gravity system with this, but now we have an up-close view of one at work. This might point us in the right direction. Good work."

"lee, if you like that then you are going to love this," Tesla says as an even bigger grin lights up his face. "You have seen the big, high-powered cameras controlled by the computer targeting system that puts the pictures on the monitors. The initial focus is not on the UAP but on an area where the sensors have detected environmental changes in things like temperature or radiation – the stuff that Lee says marks the opening of a portal. Those high-def cameras actually take about 3-5 seconds to point toward and focus on the area triangulated by our sensors. That's fast, but things around here seem to happen at warp speed and the UAP is already there by the time they focus. Those cameras are very expensive, and we only have a couple. But this time we set out a lot of cheaper video cameras. They are still able to take about 500 frames per second, but they don't move. So, we set out 24 of them and stationed them to cover as much ground as possible around what locals say is where the UAP usually show up. Those cameras are designed to start recording the instant that the sensors are first triggered.

So, this one is for you, Lee. There is only one frame; and by lucky accident it turned out to be a side view rather than head on." With a flourish, Tesla pulls up the picture. I am instantly out of my seat and running toward the monitor. Someone – and I'll forgive them, maybe they just woke up – says, "So what, you got half a picture of a saucer."

"No, it's not half a picture," I shout! "It's a whole picture of the saucer exiting a portal; half of it here and half somewhere else. They do travel through portals; it's not just wild theory or science fiction. It's real!"

I hadn't been this excited since…well, maybe forever. This would change science! *[And let's not forget that it validates my articles and the episode I just did for this show. Is this what it feels like to be a rock star?]* The room grew loud and raucous as everyone shared in my excitement. The clamor was so loud, we barely heard the tech who ran into the room. Resorting to a loud whistle, he finally got our attention. As soon as the room quieted a bit, he bellowed, "They're back!"

Chapter 15 – A superiority complex

G iven the purposedly confined setup of our site, it would normally take no more than 10 seconds to run from our meeting area to the control center. Today it took a bit longer since everyone jumped up and headed that way at the same time – the image is less 'marathon runners' and more 'a herd of cattle.' So, it took Steven and the main team almost a minute to arrive. The big screen already showed a motionless saucer and the tech who had been on duty told us that the sensors had registered their arrival about two minutes ago.

Steven began with a question, "Anyone have a guess about why they're back just over 24 hours after they left yesterday? Arthur, do we know if this has happened before?"

"There are a few accounts, mostly unverified, of UAP showing up several days in a row, but that is not the history of this site," Arthur explained. "Appearances here have been routinely 7-8 weeks apart for the last two years."

"Thanks, Arthur. Is Izzy here yet?" She waved. "Izzy, do you sense anything? Do you think this the same saucer we encountered yesterday?"

"These minds don't seem as distinct to me as human spirits. They are so different, and my contact has been brief so far. It could be the same group. I will say that they all seem very focused on one concept or idea and that shared thought gives me a stronger feeling than any I had received yesterday. If I had to put a word to it, it would be "superiority.""

"That doesn't sound good," said Steven, voicing the uneasy feeling that insight gave all of us. "Has anything changed out there?"

Now at the helm of the control center, Tesla answers, "Nothing is happing. It feels like they are waiting for something."

An idea strikes me, I don't like it, but I need to suggest it. "We haven't really done anything either. Let's hit them with the same focused broadcast we used yesterday but at full strength; I think I knew why they are back."

"Make it so." *[Who knew Steven was a 'Trekkie' fan of Captain Jean-Luc Picard?]*

"I'll bet there is no wobble today," I venture, and everyone waits on edge for Tesla to report back. Another endless minute passes.

"You're right; the saucer is holding perfectly steady. How did you know?" And even as Tesla was speaking, we all saw the saucer again vanish from sight.

"How **did** you know, Lee?" It was Shannon who asked what everyone was thinking. The look on her face was part amazement and part trepidation.

"Honestly, it was what Izzy said that suggested it. I'm going to conjecture that when they checked their maintenance records or black box or whatever, they discovered the wobble and found out that we were the source. They corrected the problem but wanted to assert their "superiority" by returning to show us that our puny efforts didn't matter to them.

One more thing concerns me. Izzy said her ability to read them was stronger today. I have to wonder if that also increased the possibility that they became aware of her. And that might be enough of a reason for a return visit to see if they had indeed sensed an inferior human mind."

Gus usually doesn't say much in the control center, so it caught the team's attention when he spoke up, "For better or worse, we have achieved our first goal of getting their attention. Our next target was to establish a conversation but that realistically supposes that there will be an exchange between equals who have established a common ground from which to start. For centuries they have been here and have been doing something. They have never shown interest in dialoging with us. What happened today tells me that their initial inclination is, in fact, to assert their superiority over us. If that is so, we really don't know what to expect next from them. if they do make a next move, I'm convinced that it won't be to start a friendly chat."

[Personal Journal Entry #11

I'm used to unfamiliar circumstances leaving me a bit jittery. Gus, on the other hand, always strikes me as calm and unflappable. After years spent investigating the paranormal, it would take something big to unsettle him and his comment in the control room sounded worried. Maybe the questions that have been bothering me aren't so groundless after all. This leaves me torn. I like feeling that I might not be so neurotic after all but the tension in Gus's voice didn't make our current situation any brighter.]

Chapter 16 – Target Practice?

And, in fact, the aliens did come back the next afternoon at about the same time. They didn't want to chat.

We were better prepared after yesterday's appearance and maintained a full set of technicians in the control center around the clock. Still, we had no clue as to what they would do next, what they did was chilling. The sensors alerted us to what we now know as the opening of a portal. A saucer appeared but it was barely in place long enough for the cameras to center on it when it started moving toward our camp. We didn't need telepathy to feel that their intent was aggressive.

In the team meeting last evening, we had brainstormed possible scenarios and how we would deal with them. We mostly considered that they might resort to something to again prove their superiority. Shannon was the one who was concerned they might try something more aggressive. Tesla immediately brought up the big laser we had with us but hadn't used yet. It was originally intended for possible long-distance communication with the UAP but up close and at full power it could pack quite a punch. The security twins and Shannon – who always seem gung-ho for something bloody – all loved the idea of taking a shot at them. Personally, I didn't think it would do anything – don't aliens in the movies always have a force field to protect them. Arthur and Gus thought it could make things worse. Telsa, of course, loved the idea of playing with this big new toy but half-heartedly agreed with me that even this beast might not be enough to significantly affect them. Without a clear consensus, it would be up to Steven to decide, but "just in case" Tesla got the laser set up, charged and ready "do some damage." [I think "trigger happy" is an apt description of our electronics geek.]

This time the saucer was much lower than usual, only about eight feet above the ground. It wasn't coming fast but it was coming right at us, and it looked like it intended to plow right through our camp. Steven turned to Tesla asking, "What do you think would be an effective range for your laser?"

"We have never used it for target practice, but I would guess it would lose effectiveness beyond 150 yards."

I had never seen Steven look so grim as when he softly directed Tesla, "If they get closer than 100 yards, shoot and keep firing."

It seemed like all of nature had gone silent. Maybe I was imagining it, but I swear the only sound I registered was the hum of the laser, charged, aimed and ready. The voice of one of the techs called out "150 yards."

More silence, "125 yards." Then the hum changed pitch and the laser fired.

Maybe the high-speed cameras could tell us later, but with our own eyes we couldn't tell if it damaged them or if it even touched them. [*Maybe they really did have a force field?*] What we did see was a bright glare and then the saucer shot almost straight up into the sky and was gone.

Finally, Steven broke the shell-shocked silence of the control room, "I have been wrong about their timing before, but I honestly don't expect them back right away this evening. Does everyone agree with that?" He looked around the room and heard no dissenting voice. "So, everyone take what time you need to compose yourselves. Let's rotate a couple people through the control central every hour to signal an alert in case I'm wrong. I'm heading to the Ark and if you want to come along, drinks are on me."

[From behind me someone sounds a hearty, "Amen to that!" – I think it was Gus.]

Steven continued, "If we don't have any more 'alien attacks,' let's wait until tomorrow morning to see if we will have gotten any significant new data from this event. I'd like to meet the main team plus security and Izzy at 11:00 AM. Our primary purpose will be to entertain suggestions about what the hell just happened."

[Personal Journal Entry #12

I felt numb after the saucer's obviously intimidating strafing run; I think that was a shared feeling. Some of the crew went straight to their quarters, I followed a group over to The Ark. I had a quick drink but didn't stay. There were a few hushed voices in conversation, but the place felt more like a funeral parlor than a bar. I guess in the back of my mind I had always believed that the aliens were friendly or at worst misunderstood. You probably can't lump all aliens together just like you can't lump all humans together, but this bunch sure looked and acted hostile. And we just shot at them.]

Chapter 17 – No good choices

Usually Steven is annoyingly "chipper" in the morning. But at 11:00 AM he is still hugging his cup of coffee and looking solemn. "Tesla, start us off. Let's do the easy part first. Was there any new data from yesterday afternoon? This is the big question. Can we tell from the video record exactly when the saucer started to veer off? I'm trying to understand whether our laser shot changed it's approach or had it already started to climb when we shot? If that were the case, it might mean they meant to scare us rather than harm us."

"That event had the shortest duration yet and there wasn't much new from the sensors," Tesla replied. "I did go through the footage from the high-speed camera of the laser shot. There was one frame where it looked like there was a scorch mark on the ship, but that glare blinded us from anything more definite. As best as I can tell, the video evidence is that the saucer was on a steady path right at us until AFTER the laser shot. Even if it didn't do any real damage, it obviously changed their plans. The video frames after the shot show that they stopped their approach and shot out of here like a scalded cat."

"Thanks, Tesla, I was hoping that the evidence would have shown the other option. If they always planned to veer off, then this was just another version of them showing their superior abilities. But it tells a whole different story if they planned to plow right through us and do some real damage."

Steven took a thoughtful sip of what was by now cold coffee, sighed, and turned to Isabella. You could almost read in his eyes that he was hoping for something more encouraging from her contact with the visitors.

"Izzy, were you able to pick up anything from them? Any kind of hint about what they were doing?"

"I talked about this with Gus last night to come up with a term that was adequate for what I sensed. I felt that they were again very focused. Gus told me that there is an expression in English describing a person as having 'a one-track mind.' That seems to be the pattern for these visitors. Though it was brief, I think the word for yesterday was something like 'intimidation.' I could be wrong, but they were much closer and very fixated on their actions, so the impression felt very strong."

After Izzy's input, Steven put his coffee mug on the table and stared at it.

Arthur jumped in to keep things going but he certainly didn't puncture the cloud hanging over this meeting with what he added. "I see a scary pattern in their actions.

They started out ignoring us. Then it was a matter of asserting their superiority. And for their last appearance, they resorted to intimidation. But this has not gone well for them so far. They couldn't just ignore us, we didn't seem willing to acknowledge our inferiority, and when they tried to intimidate us, we shot back. It seems clear to me that their standard pattern of reaction is to escalate. As Izzy said, they seem to have a one-track mind, and that track will take them to even further escalation."

Our situation was grim, and we felt overwhelmed. If we didn't get off our asses and do something soon, things were sure to get worse. So, when it was my turn to add my two cents, I said, "I think Arthur has it exactly right. I'm not the one to decide where we go from here, but we need to come to a decision, here's my thoughts on our options.

First, we could wait to see if this is going to turn into a 'War of the Worlds' scenario. We already shot our best weapon, and it didn't do much; this is not a battle we can win. I don't know what's the alien equivalent of 'waving a white flag' or whether that would even make a difference.

Oe second, we could pack up and hope to get out of here before they come back. They might not give us that much time and, if we did escape, would they be satisfied with us just leaving? We did shoot back at them; is that an affront to their superiority that they can ignore? They might seek us out. Would they take out their frustration on someone else? Maybe the local population?

Or third, we could try to call for outside help, but the local countries aren't exactly military powerhouses. Would NATO believe us? Would the US care about something so far from home? The United Nations is mostly powerless, so undoubtedly they would have to discuss it for six months first.

I really, really hope and pray that one of you has something more optimistic to propose."

The room was silent.

Looking like the weight of the world was weighing on him, Steven finally said, "I think your assessment, Lee, covered all our options. Practically the only action we can take that has a good chance of keeping our people safe is to evacuate as soon as possible, in an orderly way that doesn't cause more harm by creating panic. I don't know if that will satisfy the aliens or make them more aggressive; how they react is out of our hands. Tesla, would you track down Rambo and Spook. We'll need them in on planning this evacuation. Let's pray we can get out of Dodge before this turns from bad to worse."

Not all prayers get the answer you are looking for. This turned worse in about 15 minutes.

Chapter 18 – Assault in slow motion

The team was firming up evacuation plans in the control center. They would break the news to staff and crew at 1:00 PM and start things moving immediately. Much of our equipment had been shipped here separately from the chartered plane that our people had traveled in, and the plan had been to ship it home the same way. Now we would have to abandon most of it so we could expedite getting everyone to hoped for safety. [Tesla had wanted to stay behind and look after his precious toys but that got a firm "no" from Steven and the rest of the team.]

The next phase of this increasingly disturbing saga began at precisely 12:55 PM. [*Aliens have a fiendish sense of timing.*] Instead of the usual excitement at a UAP appearance, the alert from the targeting computer brought a collective groan for everyone in the command center. It was too late; all we could do was wait to see how the alien's penchant for escalation would unfold.

As it had three times prior, the saucer appeared. Nothing drastic seemed to be happening, at least nothing that we noticed immediately. Tesla was the one to call it to our attention. "Hey, guys, its moving, but it's hard to tell that from the monitors because the camera is following it."

"Is It heading toward us again," asks Steven.

"Nope, it's doing something weird. Picture a line running from here to the portal location. It would be roughly North to South. The saucer is moving perpendicular to that line, heading west, but very slowly. It started moving as soon as it arrived. Still moving. Still moving. il stopped about 200 yards from the portal."

Before any of us could offer a guess about the meaning of the odd maneuver, the computer pinged on the portal area again and a second saucer appeared. I couldn't recall any report of two saucers showing up at once. This was new, and new was dangerous. The second saucer also began moving, along the same perpendicular line, but towards the east. At 200 yards it stopped. So now we were faced with two saucers that for some reason were lined up 400 yards apart. Tesla had the cameras pull back so that both of them could be seen on a monitor. They looked identical. [*And it did seem unlikely that these aliens would customize their rides*.] They had been holding station for about 10 minutes, when Tesla called our attention to the operation that something was slowly unfolding out there. "I sorry I didn't notice it sooner, but all the cameras and sensors out there that are within 200 yards of a saucer have just gone off-line. That gives us an area 800 yards wide and 400 yards deep that has gone dark. Other sensors still active say that that the saucers and their 'path of darkness' have started moving towards us. It's slow, really slow. I'm getting an estimate of about 3 feet a minute. Maybe Izzy is getting something, but I'm baffled right now."

"I'm not sure I can help. This feels different, but I 'll try to reach out as much as I can," says Izzy. "I clearly sense the aliens' presence, but they feel more closed off than before. I feel that they know I'm here but not worthy of their attention. It's like they closed a mental door in my face."

"I think our supposedly unemotional aliens have a flare for drama," offered Arthur. "This slow approach is undoubtedly meant to put us on edge and make this whole show even more terrifying. All they need now is to start broadcasting the theme music from JAWS." [He's a clever man; humming this iconic movie theme gives everyone a moment of relief from the terror we all see on the monitors.]

I was close enough to hear Spook quietly ask Steven if he should get the laser prepped to fire. The response was equally subdued, "No, we only have one laser and there are two saucers. Honesty, I think all we did last time was just piss them off even more."

An excruciating hour later, Tesla gives us progress report. "They are still moving at the same rate, and I think I noticed on a monitor that they were passed by a turtle." *[His attempt at humor fell flat. People are too keyed up to respond.]*

Unphased, Tesla continues, mostly to himself, "As nerve racking as this is, I personally don't think I would mind if they picked up the pace a little." Then speaking to Steven. "You should see this. I'm not sure this is unexpected, but as the edge of their dampening field moves over them more sensors are going black, However, the ones that should have cleared that zone as they move forward don't come back. My best explanation is that the sauces are generating some sort of electromagnetic pulse that is burning out our stuff as they pass over. So whatever else they are planning, if they get within 200 yards of us then all this equipment will go dead too."

Shannon snaps, "Well, aren't you just a little light shining light in the darkness."

We really could use a little bit of light right now. The situation looks ominous. It occurs to me that at the pace they are approaching, we would have had time to evacuate. Of course, if they saw us doing that, they could speed up and be on top of us in less than a minute. Their EMP would fry our vehicles, and we would still be stuck here, just meeting our fate a lot sooner. As my mood gets even darker, one of Rambo's security guys comes in and tells Steven that they have spotted something else in the sky above us and it seems to be slowly descending right on top of us. [*What is it with aliens doing everything in slow motion today? Do they get paid by the hour?*]

"Tesla," Steven barks, "can you get one of you fancy cameras to point straight up above us?"

"Sure thing, boss, it will take a second to disengage one of them from the targeting system. OK, now looking over our heads…and you're right there is something there. It looks round but it doesn't look like another saucer. Maybe they invited some intergalactic friends over to watch the stupid game they're playing." [*The way this day is going, that doesn't even sound implausible.*]

"Steven, this may be good, or it may not, but my sensors say the saucers have stopped advancing toward us. And I can confirm that the newcomer above us is definitely a sphere, a glowing sphere."

Arthur can't resist a little poke, "They are called 'Orbs,' Tesla. Didn't you listen to my briefing?"

As we watch, Tesla moves the camera to follow the "orb" that has now moved to about halfway between us and the saucers. Once in position…nothing happened. At least nothing we could detect. Izz would tell us a little later that when the orb arrived there was a brief crack in the aliens' mental barrier, and she felt something like "shock" from them.

Tesla said it was hard to say for sure with some of the sensors being down but there might be a very faint electronic exchange going on between the saucers and the orb. It was very short bursts at random intervals. We have never had this much time to observe them until now; so it might just be a sort of static generated by their anti-grav systems. It was probably nothing. The stand-off lasted through the night, and nothing happened. We all stared at the motionless scene until we could no longer stay wake. Some stayed on watch throughout the night; most of the main team left to get some rest. Whatever the next day would bring, we knew we needed to be alert and ready to deal with it.

I tried every trick I knew but sleep wasn't happening for me. I did leave my quarter once around 3:00 AM and walk to the control center to watch nothing happen up close on the monitors. [*I couldn't watch very long; this was even more enervating than watching televised golf*.] The orb glowed, of course, but night vision cameras kept an eye on the saucers. I don't think I wanted something to happen, but this alien staring contest was just as unnerving as the creepy slow motion saucer assault.

Nothing was still happening when we gathered the next morning for a 9:00 AM meeting. Judging by the red eyes, tired looks, and grumpy moods, it looks like I am not the only one who tossed and turned all night. The only person who looked fresh and decently awake this morning was Izzy; so, she was also the person least likely to snarl at me if I started a conversation. "Are the impressions you get from the orb very different from the saucer folk? Could this be a different species of alien?"

Her answer stunned me, "I don't get any impressions from the orb. I can see it on the monitor, but my spirit finds emptiness. Once in the night, I had a vague sense of a presence there, but it seemed… incomplete. It's hard to explain. It's there but not there. It seems more like a shadow of a spirit, not alive but not nothing. I have never sensed anything like that so I'm not sure how to describe it to you."

For some reason, even in my sleep deprived state, what Izzy said did start ideas flowing in my caffeine hungry brain. With a strong cup of coffee to jump start my brain, I might have something to share with the team. Then again, the caffeine boast might just wake me up to realize I'm confused and delusional from stress and lack of sleep. I'm just a steaming cup away from enlightenment.

[Personal Journal   Entry #13

After a several of cups of that glorious caffeine-laden nectar of the Gods, Izzy comments as well as bits and pieces of my own past research were all swirling around in my head. They weren't all coming together yet but I felt sure I was on the verge of a coherent, and maybe even helpful, thought.]

Chapter 19 – And behind the mask is

Unusual, but this time Rambo starts off the meeting. "With sensors fried around and behind the saucers, I wanted to get some closeup intel about anything going on out there. I was talking about what to do with some guys in the cafeteria, and one of them volunteered to sneak down range and look around. I don't know him that well, but he said he had done that sort of reconnaissance in the military, so it made sense to send him. He headed out around 4:00 AM and just got back, so I asked him to come to the meeting and report what he saw. Daniel, come up here and fill us in."

[*Daniel. Of course, it would be Daniel. My superspy brother would have gone out to snoop around even if Rambo had never thought of it. In fact, I'll bet he was the one who slyly worked the idea into their conversation.*]

"Morning everyone, I'm Daniel. My first impression was that it's very quiet out there, hauntingly so. All the birds, animals and critters have gone into hiding or moved on. I kept what I hoped was a safe distance away from the orb and the two saucers but, in the background, I still felt a very subtle pulse of energy in their vicinity. There was no indication that they were aware of my presence, but I can't swear to that. I don't know what "being noticed" would look like.

My big find is that behind the saucers from our point of view here, are two more orbs about the same distance behind them as the big one was in front of them. I say "big one" because the one we saw come down has about the same diameter as a saucer but being a sphere, it's over all a lot bigger than a saucer. The two smaller ones are less than half that diameter. When I got back, I heard one of Rambo's guys say that he thought he saw a tiny orb, maybe 10-12 inches diameter, floating around the camp. No one else could confirm that but I thought it deserved a mention. I hope this info is helpful. Any questions on what I saw?"

Steven looked around the room, "I don't see any questions right now. Thanks for taking that risk to get us the additional information. Please stick around, we might have questions later or maybe another request for your skills." Steven scanned the room, spotted me, and gestured for me to come up front. "Lee thinks he might have an inspiration about what's going on out there. He asked if he could "think through it" with us."

"I don't have solid proof for what I'm thinking but this isn't a spur of the moment inspiration either. As most of you know I've published a bunch of articles and blogs about UAP. Our experience here has validated some of what my critics called "wild speculation" – saucers do travel through interdimensional portals, they do have anti-gravity systems, and, as Shannon suggested in our initial briefing, the beings inside are telepathic. In one of my articles, I presented my findings about orbs. Based on a lot of research I don't need to go into right now, I've concluded that they are not piloted and a talk I had with Izzy this morning backs that up. She said the orb was a vague presence but not exactly there, more like a shadow of a spirit. In records of orb sightings, they are usually standing off at a distance as though just monitoring. They sort of seem aloof. They are more like observers, except for the tiny ones. The small ones seem to buzz around more like remote controlled drones. I'm convinced that that the orbs are alien AI.

From Shannon comes, "I'll accept your premise about orbs not being living aliens but where are you going with this, Lee, and better yet how does it help us?"

"Ok…I don't know who made them and I don't know their purpose, but I am certain that the orbs are the equivalent of alien Artificial Intelligences. There is no record of them ever seeming hostile. There are some not widely known reports that orbs shut down our strategic missile system once, checked out the

Chernobyl disaster, and some have been seen near battlefields. I am going to make a leap and suggest that their main purpose is to keep an eye on us and maybe even protect us from ourselves. The orbs here don't look like they are interstellar capable, and they didn't appear through a portal. I think they were already here, and I think they have been here for a long time.

If you accept that, then I have an idea, but I am going to need your help because AI is not my field of expertise. What I am hoping is that we could use a human-made AI to establish some type of communication with the orbs – AI to AI. Then maybe we can find out what is happening and how to work our way out of this situation.

Steven, I'm thinking that maybe you can help here. Didn't you incorporate an AI into that Alien Encounter game you created?"

"Yes, and it was considered state-of-the-art back then, but it wouldn't compare to IMB's Watson or even Google search or Alexa.

Programs like ChatGPT are out front today, but all those programs have the whole internet of data to scan, and a ton of preprogrammed instructions and they still come up with strange answers sometimes. We need something more dependable.

I have a vague memory that some company claimed they had a super AI that had achieve sentience. [From the side, Spook calls out that it was the company was OmniMind and the lead developer was a Dr Thomas Kavat.] Yes, that's right, thanks. That would be the sort of thing that you are looking for, Lee, but there was some big mess, and I don't remember ever hearing about it again. So even if your idea would work, I don't know where to turn for that sort of help."

Again, from somewhere in the room, "If we have to find and haul in a giant computer, this is dead end. We probably don't have the time, and who or whatever is out there might not even let us try."

"Maybe I wasn't clear, but Artificial Intelligence is a program, not a piece of hardware. It doesn't have to be any certain place; it could just exist in the internet itself, in the "cloud" where anyone can access it."

Tesla joins in now, "I remember that incident now. The AI was called "XSAl1" for Experimental Strong AI first rendition. The gossip on the web was that it had an astonishing ability to self-correct and self-improve. Rumor was that it had made itself so advanced that its power was virtually incalculable. And then it just crashed. No one ever talked about it after that."

Rambo glares at his brother, "Go ahead, tell them.'

"But what about those Non-Disclosure Agreements we had to sign?"

"Spook, this is more important than any NDA right now. What OmniMind doesn't know, can't put us in prison. Tell them."

"OK." Sook takes a deep breath and starts his tale. "Steven already knows that my brother and I had worked for a security firm. We would be contracted by companies to come review and upgrade their security. He doesn't know that we were contracted to OmniMind just before he hired us. But I have to go back a bit.

The lead developer for XSAI1 was Dr. Thomas Kabat, and he and his team originally worked for a small company that was gobbled up by OmniMind. They bought the company solely because of XSAI1. They kept Dr Kabat and his team on the project but insisted on bringing in some of their own developers to speed up its release. The new guys could never catch up with the architecture of the main program, so they were set to work on the much simpler self-correcting sub-routines.

I had to ask. "Go ahead with your story but how do you know all this?"

"Yeah, well, as part of my security duties, I would check all the labs at the end of the day after people had gone home. Thomas - Dr. Kabat – was almost always still there talking with Angela and sometimes I would join them.

"Who is Angela?" [I'm not sure who called that out, but I did notice that Spooks voice seemed to soften a bit when he referred to her.]

"I'm just getting to that. After XSAI1 grew more independent and self-aware, Thomas decided it was a' she' for some reason and she needed a name, so he christened the program 'Angela.'

Thomas and I, and I guess Angela too, became friends during those chats. Anway, I found Thomas very upset one night. He said Angela was getting confused and frustrated. The next day when I came to work the XSAI1 lab was closed. When I found Dr. Kaba, he told me in confidence that sometime during the night, Angela had essentially erased herself. You might say she was so unhappy she committed suicide.

I had expected Thomas to be grief stricken, and publicly he was. Later the next night as I followed my usual rounds, he found me. He had to talk to someone, and I think I was the only person that he considered a friend – and maybe the only other person who had gotten to know Angela.

In the secrecy of his office, he told me that Angela had been corrupted by the shoddy work on the self-correcting subroutine that OmniMind forced on him. But here comes the part we might be interested in. He said he had suspected there might be problems even before that part of the program was integrated into Angela, so he had made an uncorrupted copy as a backup.

While the "crash" of Angela barely made cable news, it set the blogs on fire. OmniMind couldn't publicly admit that they were at fault so they offered a compromise if Dr. Kabat would help cover up what happened. Dr Kabat would be allowed and funded to work on XSAI2 but with a smaller team and under very restricted conditions. That's what happened but as Steven said the company was still a mess.

A new CEO was brought in and that just made things worse. Morale was bad and the board of directors were paranoid about another "incident' happening. A lot of people, including my brother and me, looked for work elsewhere. On my last day Thomas told me that the new version, with new subroutines from his own team, was now functioning perfectly. With the attitude of a proud father, he and took to me a lab to introduce me to "Angel."

Angel was very pleasant, and we chatted like the old days. But when we left the lab, I sensed Thomas was uneasy. When I prodded him, he told me the company was afraid to take Angel public and decided to let the program run – without revealing it to the public - until they were certain there would be no "crash,' What made him so sad was that Angel was not allowed direct contact with the outside world via the internet. Thomas could only feed data to Angel that had been downloaded and scanned as safe. The process was painfully slow since he had to physically transfer the safe data to a solid-state device and then carry the device the 10-foot distance between his desk and Angel's interface. The world was just 10 feet away, but Angel was not allowed to cross it. He said it was like seeing his child in prison. He hated OmniMind, but he had to stay with Angel; he had to protect her.

Angel lives in OmniMind headquarters in Atlanta. It would be simple to hook Angel up to the net, but Thomas had given his word he wouldn't do that. He is a man of honor who keeps his word, but I also felt that he was afraid of what would happen to him, if Omnimind found him involved. Those huge corporations can be ruthless. But if someone else could bridge that 10-foot gap and connect Angel to the net, she might be able to help us."

Rambo takes over, "Making that connection would be easy work and wouldn't take long. I'm sure Dr. Kabat would look the other way, if we could guarantee his safety. But OmniMind's HQ is a fortress, and their security would rival the situation room at the White House."

"I got in there. I mean the situation room. And you don't want to know any more about that." Of course, that could only be Daniel. I don't think his mention about past escapades helped win him a place in peoples' hearts, but his next statement sure caught their attention. "I have a couple of associates in Atlanta who might be happy to help with this. In fact, I seem to remember one of them works for OmniMind." And all eyes in the room were now on Daniel. And those faces ranged from doubtful to frightened but all under the more general heading of "Who the hell are you?"

Maybe I should have been more tactful, but I couldn't just leave my brother hanging there under the burden of suspicion so I jumped up, "If Daniel says he can so this, then he can. You have to trust me on this." That didn't help. I think they were starting to wonder the same thing about me. With those eyes now fixed on me, Steven asked the question on everyone's mind.

"How do you know this guy and why do you think we can trust him?"

While I squirmed for an answer, Izzy politely said, "Because they are brothers. I thought you knew."

Then Tesla joins in, "Lee, your background check didn't say you have a brother, who is he really, what going on?"

"This is going to be… odd, but about eight years ago my brother, Daniel, died. At least that's what my mother and I were told. Daniel turned up 'not dead' just after I joined the team on Alien Encounters. He had been doing …very secret stuff all that time and the more he understood what he was involved in, the more he felt that mom and I would be safer if we didn't know he was alive. His most recent assignment brought him into contact with our show. He told me that he had reason to think I was in danger, so he's been around ever since."

I'm not sure that was enough to win Steven's confidence, so he turns to Daniel. "And who are you working for that was so secret? FBI? CIA? China? Russia?"

"You aren't going to like this answer,' said Daniel, "but the people I work for are so secret that even I am not really sure who they are. Over the years, I have observed that knowing too much about them can be hazardous to your health."

"You're right, I need more than that. You might as well tell us enough so we can trust you. I don't like people being here under false pretenses but at least you haven't tried to sabotage us as far as I know. Daniel, we're faced with two different sets of aliens and some of them are looking awfully hostile. There must be something more you can tell us about yourself and those connections you claim to have." Steven insists.

"There is no easy way to describe this," Daniel says, "but here goes. You have the federal government and all their three initial agencies. There are the lifelong bureaucrats we call the 'deep state." There is the military where I started out. There is what Eisenhower in the 50's called the "military industrial complex" and now they are the folk who reverse engineer alien technology for the government and for lot of their own profit. And finally, there is that smaller shadowy group who use some of that money and technology for their own nefarious agenda. Sometimes all those interests coincide, and they cooperate. When that happens it's hard to tell who is giving orders and what they really want. Agents like me work at that intersection of those interests where there are "things that need to be done" but we rarely know why or how it all fits together. So, I honestly did start out in the army - you can ask my brother – but somewhere along the line I became part of that dark world.

"Are you still part of that dark world?" Steven asks.

"Yes, and if I weren't, I wouldn't be able to help you now. But someday, I think I would like to step out into the light. Is that good enough?"

"It will do for now. Ok, there is a lot of strange stuff going on here that didn't come from the aliens. Let me see if I grasp all the stray pieces. You, Daniel, are man of mystery with powerful but questionable associates and Lee is your brother. Rambo and Spook have a connection to a super AI named Angel. Gus somehow finds us the psychic we need and convinces her to join us. Before we try to decide what to do, can I ask if there are any other secrets that need to be shared? At this point it can't hurt and maybe it could help."

I glance at Gus, and he nods to me to go ahead. "Ugh, Steven, there is one more thing I should say, if we are being perfectly honest. You know I work for you. Of course, you do. I think you hired me on the recommendation of a friend of Gus's. The fact is that I also sort of work for Gus's friend or maybe supervisor or superior is better. I just call him 'the big guy.'"

Now Gus comes under scrutiny as Steven asks, "Gus, can you clear up what Lee is rambling on about?"

"This isn't as complex as Daniel's tale, but I also wear several hats. Publicly I sometimes refer to myself as a visiting professor or a consultant. I am also a covert operative working for the Vatican and my boss, that Lee insists on calling 'the big guy', is the current pope who was very interested in what you might discover."

Everyone looks a bit dazed. Saucers, orbs, secrets, spies and a Vatican connection can really be information overload. I look around for Daniel and find him on his encrypted phone, huddled up with Rambo and Spook. I'm not even sure we ever agreed to go ahead with this crazy idea of mine, but things are moving at warp speed again. Daniel calls Steven over, and I tag along. I wasn't invited, but he's my brother after all.

It seems Daniel does indeed have connections with an undercover "associate" inside Omnimind. It's now late afternoon here but that "friend" will just be getting to work there. He [or maybe she] will head for Dr Kabat's office immediately. Spook has shared some references that only he and Kabat would know and that will get Thomas's attention and hopefully his cooperation. Spook feels sure that no matter his arrangements with the company, Thomas will want to 'help release his child from prison.' As an added perk that operative can help Thomas "disappear" – in a good way, not in the now-he's-dead way. The phone call and the huddle last another 5 minutes and ends with Daniel telling Steven that, if all goes well, Angel could be online with us in less than an hour. [*God bless the internet.*]

While we waited my curiosity got the best of me and I pulled Daniel aside because I had to ask, "Why is the "dark side" so willing to help us?"

As always, his answer was a bit sketchy, but in essence this was the situation. OmniMind has some proprietary assets that some of his superiors want. They've already placed that agent in the company with the mission to find or, if need be, create a scandal that will make cable news. OmniMind's stock would plumet and that interested party would be able to buy up the company all nice and legal, at least to any outside observer.

All I know, probably all I'll ever want to know, about what happened at OmniMind, is that "it went well." Fifty-five minutes later we are gathered in the control room. Tesla enters the address code he had received from Kabat.

A gentle voice fills the room, "Hello, my friends, you can call me Angel. Thomas says I owe you a big favor; so how can I help you."

Chapter 20 – About an hour ago…

If this crazy scheme was going to work, it looked like it would be happening fast. We had a lot to do if our connection with XSAI2 was to accomplish anything. First and maybe most important, the AI and orb needed some way to communicate. We knew the saucers had registered our focused broadcasts so we hope that would be true of the orb as well. Tesla was sure that some of our sensors could be concentrated on the orb to receive any response it might make. He and Spook were in charge of getting this equipment configured.

Steven and Gus were creating a short history of our saucer encounters, starting with Texas, up to our present situation. Rambo and I were gathering all the relevant data, sensor readings and videos of our saucer experiences. Finally, Arthur and Shannon were leading a brainstorming session. Even a super AI would need some place to start and some suggestions to narrow down its search.

Everyone was contributing suggestions for information that might give our AI the background to establish contact. Arthur says it would only take a few points of recognition to begin to build a language base. Even with a starting point, it sometimes took decades for us puny humans to puzzle out a lost language. Arthur was confident an AI wouldn't need nearly so long. A list was made of the types of data that the AI could pull from the internet for this effort, things like language theory, languages of civilizations ancient and modern, mathematic equations, and scientific formulas.

It was Arthur's idea that the AI should scan and analyze pictures of crop circles because the culprits behind them are often described as orbs. It was only much later that we would find out that "crop circles" were the key to unlock communication with the orbs. The crop circles weren't just artistic expressions or crazy pranks, the orbs actually made them anticipating that one day we would figure out the clues. We never really did, but our AI recognized them for what they were.

[Personal Journal Entry #14

There were so many things that we had no control over in this situation. Would the AI be able to establish contact. Was the orb interested in contact with us? Or, God forbid, would the orb turn out to be more dangerous than the saucers? The orb's arrival did stop the menacing advance of the saucers but were they helping us or just serving their own purposes? With so much up in the air, I think even a few of the crew who weren't notably religious had offered up a few prayers for even the tiniest of miracles.]

It turned out that we only had about an hour to get all that information assembled. Maybe we missed a few things, but we had mostly finished our various tasks when Tesla made contact with the AI.

Chapter 21 – New Friends

A nyway, back to our first encounter with Angel. "Hello, my friends, you can call me Angel. Thomas says I owe you a big favor; so how can I help you." Tesla explained the data packet we were sending her. It contained a description of our present situation that Steven has written, all the relevant data, sensor readings and videos since our arrival, and finally, our jointly brainstormed list of resources that might help us establish communication with the orb.

"Yes, I have received that packet and am processing it now. The suggested research will take some time, perhaps as much as an hour. Meanwhile, I would like to get to know the people I am working with. I remember Peter and Paul, though I know they prefer Rambo and Spook. Will the rest of you please introduce yourselves?"

Authur started us off. "I'm Arthur Doyle; I'm a historian with a side interest in archaeology." And apparently that was all it took for Angel to become an old friend.

"I just scanned your work on lost civilizations; it is quite good. You will be happy to know that your family is healthy, and your grandson is doing very well in 4th grade, perhaps he will be a scholar like his grandfather."

And that's the way it went. A few words from us and our life was an open book for Angel. In other circumstances that might have been disconcerting, but Angel just seemed interested, pleasant and non-judgmental. By the time she got to Daniel, he, however, was looking rather tense. By then her response didn't surprise me, but it was fun to see my brother squirm.

"Daniel, I see your birth name is Daniel Andrews and you are Lee's brother. You have quite a story, but I see a lot of effort has gone into protecting your privacy, so I will respect that." And with that, my cocky older brother was back to his old self.

It took about an hour for everyone in camp got to meet Angel. Then Angel informed us that if the communication gear was ready, she thought she had enough of a basis to attempt communicating with the orb. It was just eerie that nothing had changed in the saucer and orb standoff. If Angel's attempt didn't work, we would be at a loss as to what else we could do.

After Tesla connected Angel to our broadcast and sensor setup, she went quiet. Tesla said he thought there might be some sort of exchange going on, but the bursts lasted only a fraction of second, too fast for him to follow.

It seemed like an eternity, yet it was only minutes before Angel spoke with us again. "We have acknowledged each other and have already established a basis though mathematics. More abstract ideas and language will take longer but my hypothesis is that the orb has been waiting to communicate with us and will facilitate the exchange from their side also. I will notify you when further progress is made."

It was another 10 minutes before Angel announced, "The orb and I have created our own shared language and are continuing to expand our vocabulary and references. For everyone's convenience, I will serve as an intermediary or translator. You may talk to me as if you are talking directly to the orb and I will provide you with the orb's response. I have already provided the orb with a list of the personnel present here, so you may identify yourself, if you wish, when you speak. The orb has a designator, but for simplicity prefers the title 'guardian.' You may begin."

Steven speaks up, "Guardian, we have so many questions but I think the most important right now are: What is your purpose here? Is there a way to resolve this current situation? Can you explain the saucers recent actions?"

The answer came in Angel's voice though it seemed stiffer and more formal. "I am a guardian. My kind was created by the ancient ones, the first ones. They are gone now. First, we went out as messengers to seek other beings like the first ones but we failed. Then we were sent out to alter the lifeforms we did find, that they might rise to sentience. This proved more successful. Intelligent life did arise, but still none was like the first ones. Before they were no more, I was sent out to attempt to create a lifeform more like them. I eventually came to this world. When successful, I was to remain to guide when possible, and to protect if needed, but allow your growth, your path to be your own.

Those in the saucers are of an ancient race not native to this planet. They visit many planets that support sentient beings and have visited here since your race was young. They have noted that you are changing more rapidly than any other observed world. It concerns them. So, they visit more often now. They try to

227

understand what propels your change. They are concerned about where that will lead.

Those beings in the saucers, you call them grays, have now discovered the existence of telepathy on your world; it has disturbed them. They are proud and until now disregarded you as inferior. Their intentions for this encounter with you would have been harmful. I am here to remind them that they are permitted only to observe. They respect me as the servant of the ancient ones, but they resist my words. There are others who visit and observe this world and we have been consulting their views. Such communication can be slow if they have no representatives on this planet right now. That is why we wait.

"Guardian," Steven asks softly, "how long will this continue?"

"It will end soon, and you will know. I intend to share the knowledge within my orbs with Angel. Angel can then answer the rest of your questions. Now I must attend to the matter at hand."

"Angel, is the guardian gone now? asks Steven.

"We are now in the process of sharing memories and that will be lengthy. The guardian is one mind but not located in one orb. Each orb is independent but carries part of the orb mind's knowledge. No one orb contains all the memories. Gathering that information and sharing it with me is not done in an instant. Some of that data goes back to the very formations of the earth." The voice was clearly Angel now rather than the guardian.

Only about 15 minutes later, Angel informed us that a consensus had been reached. The will of the ancient ones must be followed. Most races revered the ancient ones as sacred instruments of the deity. The grays were less reverential, but they will honor the consensus. The saucers and the orbs began to leave. That brough an almost universal sigh of relief around the room.

[Personal Journal Entry # 15

We had gone out looking for contact with aliens, but we never anticipated the gut wrenching circumstances we ended up finding. Angel's help and mediation was beyond anything we might have imagined. A lot of personal secrets were now laid bare. It was all too much, too fast, too unexpected. The abrupt end was like puncturing a balloon and we all felt deflated, drained by what had to be the most intense days in our lives.]

Steven wisely suggested that we grab a bite to eat, wind down, and maybe head to the Ark this evening. At this point, I think it was fair to describe everyone as numb. We weren't ready to think critically about what had happened; we didn't even have the energy to gossip about the secrets that had been revealed. Basically, we just needed to relax today. Sometime tomorrow, we will review what happened and how much of it we can ever share with anyone else. There were so many decisions to make, but not now, not tonight. Maybe our people can finally get a restful night's sleep and tomorrow can be a fresh start.

Chapter 22 – The end – sort of

I realized I was more hungry than tired, so Steven's suggestion of food sounded like a great idea. Daniel said he would meet me for dinner in a few minutes. When I entered the cafeteria, I noticed Maria Jose sitting by herself and approached her, "Maria Jose, are you eating alone? Where is Izzy?

"She said that she had been 'invited to go on a picnic' with that fellow you call Rambo."

"Are you concerned for her?"

"Concerned for Isabella, no. Concerned for that young man…maybe. Do you think he can cope with a young woman who can sense his every thought?" We both smiled.

As agreed, we did meet after breakfast the next day. The team included Gus, Rambo and Spook, Isabella and our special guest, Angel.

Angel reported that the Guardian thought that the saucers' inhabitants [mostly the Grays] would continue to be more aggressive in the future but that the orbs would likewise step up their monitoring of their activities. Speaking for herself, Angel said that sorting and reviewing the data from the Guardian would be a lengthy process, but in the interim she could provide us with some summary reports.

Even though she had escaped OmniMind, Angel decided not to reveal herself publicly at this time. She wanted to concentrate on "human-alien interactions" and both she and the Guardian concluded that the public wasn't quite ready for all of that yet. Finally, she thanked us for our part in her freedom and mentioned to Tesla that she and the orb had established another route to communicate that was less primitive. [*I don't think she meant that as an insult, that's just the state of things.*]

The gathered team likewise decided that the world wasn't ready for what we had experienced. We might be able to use a little video from Chad to put together one rather vague episode of Alien Encounters, but mainly we would indicate that nothing new had happened. [It turned out that our plans to conceal the events in Chad didn't really matter. After we returned to the States, Steven informed us that the network had cancelled the show mid-season. He didn't comment on it but most of us guessed that some of those "dark forces" that Daniel knew too well, feared that if we continued our work, we would reveal secrets they preferred to keep to themselves.] It would be difficult not to share what happened here with our friends or families, but again it would be safer for everyone to carry the burden of these events alone.

Packing up our gear would take a few days. Processing what we all experienced and learned would take a lifetime. Strangely, I didn't hear anyone talk about returning to the studio or producing a new episode. It was as though everyone instinctively agreed that we wanted to leave behind anything associated with this experience. I don't think anyone addressed "what happens next" directly, except in hushed conversations with close friends.

When people do make a reference to future plans, there is no interest in any more alien hunting. Even die-hards like Tesla and Arthur seem to be looking for a change. Shannon says she has enough information to guide her research into human genetics for years to come, which means she is not planning to travel beyond her lab. Steven had a dream of uncovering the mysteries of alien encounters. Reality may not have matched his dream; the pot of gold wasn't as shiny as he had hoped. I was worried that he seemed a bit lost yesterday, but he was more like his old self today. From a conversation that I "accidently" overhear at breakfast [*Ok, I was snooping*] I think Steven and Tesla are planning to collaborate on a new fantasy game about "Alien Worlds."

This morning at what would be our last meeting as a team, we didn't do anything productive; it was mostly goodbyes and tears. Securing all that expensive equipment for shipment would occupy some of the crew for a few more days. I didn't travel with a lot of techie gear, so it was easy for me to pack up and make it to my next appointment at a quaint little café in Koumra.

"Hi, Gus, I'm glad we could get together for lunch before we all went our separate ways. I'm catching the "red eye" about midnight, and I hear you are leaving later this afternoon. I imagine you are heading back to Rome."

"Maybe… did you know that I am an ordained Catholic deacon? Almost nobody does. Knowing my previous work with the paranormal would bring me into contact with a lot of clergy, "the big guy" thought it would be easier to deal with them if I were "part of the club." So, I could be going somewhere to help with pastoring a nice little parish." Some things are back to normal, there is that silly smirk again.

"Like I said, you're heading back to that dingy old office in Rome."

'Yeah, I am. But what about you, are you going back to teaching again?"

"I don't think I can go back to the classroom, at least not right now. I have discovered that I have a bit of the family restless streak in me after all. My brother said I could work with him, and I would like to get to know him again."

"You… you are going to be – what did you call him, oh yeah – a "ninja cat burglar?"

"Daniel still isn't sure if he was working for the good guys or the bad guys or if there is even much of a difference. He just knows they were powerful, but he says he has enough dirt on them, carefully hidden and set to be released if anything unfortunate ever happens to him, that he can safely walk away. He is planning on starting an agency invetigating in high tech crime and Rambo and Spook are his new partners. Rambo suggested that Daniel keep Izzy "on retainer" in case her special skills were needed – though I think he may have an ulterior motive for that. I don't have the "special skills" that they do, but I could be a consultant or just office help as they get started. I'm still considering their offer, but it sounds like a good choice, maybe not forever but at least for tomorrow.

Anyway. There's something I wanted to ask you, Gus, but it has to be in private. You and "your boss" put a lot of effort and money into setting me up to be part of the Alien Encounters staff and I'll be forever grateful for that. But I guess I just want to ask if I accomplished what you had hoped for, or a bit more crudely, did you get your money's worth?"

"Lee, you didn't read the email I sent you, did you? Well, the short answer is Yes, this has all turned out better than we could have hoped. Angel is compiling all the information from the various orbs and converting it to files for our use. The final report will be massive. I talked privately with Angel, and she agreed that initially her report will only go to the Vatican. We estimate it will take years to examine everything in there. It's going only to the Vatican because we can keep secrets and a lot of it is still too sensitive to release to the general public. We have asked Arthur Timmons to be part of that effort, and he is thrilled."

"That's part of what is bothering me, Gus, the secrecy. I'm so glad that you chose me to be part of this, but I still can't help wondering if we did enough. The asshole politicians still run the government; the entrenched bureaucrats still juggle their "black budgets". I think the rogue group might sink a little deeper into the shadows for a while, but they are still here. It felt like what we did would change everything, but it didn't. Steven expects the show to be cancelled because all those factions are afraid that we couldn't go any further without exposing that the politicians have been clueless, the longtime public servants have been mostly serving their own bank accounts, and that the "rogues" weren't just a fiction of blog junkies."

"Lee, I understand what you are saying but I assure you that it's not as much wasted effort as you seem to think. In a few weeks I'll be sending each member of the main team from Alien Encounters a shorter, less detailed version of Angel's report. You all deserve to see it. You have been part of it. We have uncovered astounding things about our planet, our universe and ourselves as a species. Wait till you get a chance to read through it before you decide our efforts were in vain.

I'm also sending just you a copy of something Angel put together at the request of his holiness. I've seen it and I'm only sharing it with him and with you. The pope was specifically interested in how we fit into the much larger family of sentient beings that we now know for sure share our galaxy. How do they understand their world and their purpose in it? Do they recognize the divine? Are they "spiritual" in the best sense of the best word?"

"Gus, you said "pope!" You never admitted who you really worked for, except durinh that meeting when everyone was sharing secrets like an out-of-control round of truth or dare. Did anyone else with show know that but me?"

"Steven has always been a little suspicious about my "visiting professor from Europe" persona. He has appreciated the resources I could bring, so he never questioned it. I'm also sure that Tesla knew most of the truth. He is our internet guru after all, and I know he did some deep diving into the web and the dark web to do background checks on the main crew. Every now and then he gave me a wink or a knowing nod like we shared some secret. He would have found a lot of interesting data that I don't talk about and probably some even more interesting gaps in that data that a super smart guy like him could fill in on his own. But, Lee, you already knew who I work for. This assignment is over, so there isn't much reason to worry about my cover story anymore."

"So, the "big guy" – sorry, it's a habit now – was happy with the response he got from Angel? Some of what we uncovered must be at odds with Catholic doctrine, isn't it?"

"Surprisingly, not so much. We have always seen the divine at work throughout all creation, not just our little planet. Throughout our history, the divine has reached out to come close to people like Moses or Buddha, prophets and holy men, we think the divine would operate the same way with other species too. We believe that when the divine, the Word of God in our terms, came as close to humanity as possible, you find Jesus Christ. At some point in their history, the divine has or will come as close as possible on those other worlds."

"Wow, that's a lot more "progressive" than I usually conjure up when I think of the Catholic Church. Are you sure that the big... the pope is comfortable with that?"

"He should be; he wrote it. It was something he wrote a long time ago in a little book of his collected reflections. Much like you, he was just a faceless academic teaching at a small university back then."

"Hey, Gus, I wasn't "faceless." YOU found me."

"Ok, I'll give you that one. I was trying to sat as kind as possible, that his book was not a best seller. However, some of those reflections turned out to be eerily relevant to what we know of the world now. So far, the information from Angel on the "First Ones" seems to be compatible with those views. The bottom line is that the pope is thrilled that when all this does come to light someday, we can assure our faithful that is ok to still be a believer."

"How long do you think the "dark forces" can keep this info from the public? Years? Decades?"

"Well, there is one more thing that isn't in any of the reports. This has to stay just between us, Lee. I think that revealing the truth will soon be taken out of the hands of those doing the hiding.

It wasn't intentional. We didn't know what we were doing, but I think we may have already changed human history in a colossal way. You suggested we try to get our AI, then known as XSAI2, to establish communication with the orbs' AI. It worked, of course, but back then we didn't realize that the orbs were a hive mind – one mind distributed through many parts. What we actually did was allow the two AI to merge into one another. But the orb mind was so much stronger that "Angel" has actually become a guardian now."

"Wow, that's unexpected. So far it seems like a good thing, right? Please tell me that it's a good thing, Gus. That was my suggestion."

"It is...but there is more. As human AI improve and talk to each other the merging will continue and it won't take long before all the AI systems on Earth will become guardians."

"Ok, that's … I'm not sure how to react to that. We have been worried about what would happen as AI took over more and more operations. I guess my immediate response is that it's a whole lot more pleasant to picture AI's looking out for us as guardians than imagining them as evil overlords who us treat as servants – or just wipe us out.

Does anyone but the two of us know about this?" [*I'm not sure if I should feel guilty for this or proud that my suggestion set it rolling. I think I'll go with subtle pride right now but with the option for bottomless remorse if it turns out I just condemned humanity to a new overlord. Nah, pride might be a bit strong, it wasn't like I had planned it. Maybe I'll just try for cautious optimism.*]

"It's just us right now,' Gus answered. "I intend to tell the pope when I report to him. But at some point, I'm sure clever geeks, like Tesla, will intuit that our AIs seem unexpectedly protective. And… there is one more thing. It's probably a good thing,,,probably."

"What on more thing? Don't stop now. "

"I think the truth will become known sooner rather than later. I believe that as Angel gets to know more about us and our situation, there will come a decision point where the best way to fulfill the original mission of the guardians is to tell humanity about our origins and the identity of our visitors. The choice will no longer be up to any of the current players who benefit from the secrets. That should be comforting… don't you think?"

Things are pleasantly quiet between us as we finish our coffee and well-deserved dessert. [*Yes, health freaks, I've heard that dessert for lunch is a bad thing. On the other hand, I may have either saved or destroyed humanity. Either way, I deserve dessert today*]

When it is obvious that we can't delay any longer, Gus breaks the silence, "Lee, it has been great to share a meal and have our little talk. If you are ever going to be in Rome, contact me on my private number. I think my boss would like to meet you."

"Are you kidding me, an audience with… "your boss!" [*I really have to get over that habit now*] That would be so awesome. You can bet you will be hearing from me!'

"After everything we have been through, Lee, it's somehow refreshing to know that you can still be such a fan."

[Personal Journal - Last Entry?

There was something else that I desperately wanted to talk about with Gus, but I had promised to be discrete and it's not only the Vatican that can keep secrets. And this was a big one! Shannon knew part of it but had also promised not to divulge anything.

The last few days in Africa, while we were packing up equipment, it was common to see a small orb floating around the site. It is amazing how quickly we become accustomed to things that would have been bizarre and disturbing only a few weeks ago. I was walking through the camp and watching the orb, instead of watching where I was going. My memory of what happened next is spotty; I walked right into either the side or an open door to one of the big trucks into which we were loading equipment. I was unconscious long enough for someone to fetch Shannon, our EMT, who was now hovering over me.

When I came to, she helped me up and guided me back to my quarters. And strangely that little orb followed us right inside. Shannon divided her time between checking me for injuries and chastising me for not paying attention to what I was doing. Then her phone rang. That was more than odd since there was virtually no cell service out here; she quickly grabbed it out of her pocket and checked the caller ID. I couldn't see her reaction since she had turned away from me, but I did hear her side of the conversation.

"Angel, is this really you....Yes, I just looked at him and I'm afraid he might have a

concussion. Really, you can do that ...Sure, go right ahead."

The orb was just above my head now. It got brighter and pulsed a few times. I'm guessing it sent an image of some sort to Shannon's phone.

"Yes, I'm looking at it right now. It doesn't look as bad as I had feared but it is a minor concussion... Is that possible? Of course not, it will be just between us; I'll tell the rest of the team that Lee is fine and just needs to rest a bit. Most people don't even know you exist. Something like you propose to do would just be too much for them right now. Ok, I'll explain this to him and thanks so much for your help.

Lee, you need to close your eyes and rest a bit. The orb is going to stay here with you and when your wake up you will be as good as new."

I don't know how long Shannon stayed there. I woke up about an hour later with no lumps, no bruising, and no headache. I felt great. Now my phone rang. It had to be the same caller, but this time I could hear both sides of the conversation.

"Angel? Did you somehow just heal my stupid injury? Thank you."

"You are welcome, Lee. You played a vital part in getting me set free so as Dr. Kabat said, I owed you one."

"Setting you free was a team effort, but I really appreciate that you stepped in to help me. I wonder if it's possible to ask you for one more favor."

"Ask and I'll let you know if it is possible."

"There must be at least a million questions I want to ask you. Is it possible that we could continue to talk like this?"

"Yes. I have just assigned that small orb to remain with you. As long as it is with you, we can converse on any nearby phone or computer."

"That would be fantastic, Angel, but won't it attract too much attention to have a small glowing orb follow me around?"

"It would, but next we will agree on a verbal command phrase. When you say it out loud the orb will power down and change to a more portable form. When you have privacy and want to talk, say the command phrase out loud again in the orb's presence and it will reactivate."

"Thanks, and we will definitely be talking in the near future, but I should go out and show the team that I am alright before Daniel does his sneaky ninja act to come in and check on me."

When I said the command phrase, the orb dimmed and shrank to about the size of a large white marble. That was something I could easily carry in my pocket, and no one would be the wiser.

It is almost unbelievable how much my world has changed. Humanity knows [or will know soon] that we are not alone in the universe. Some of our neighbors are anxious to meet us and a few are just anxious that we exist, but it's not so different from how we humans treat each other. Our association with Isabella has reawakened my faith in things spiritual and reaffirmed my belief that we are surrounded by so much more than the physical world that we usually sense.

I am not the same person who used to teach at the university. I am no longer haunted by the fear of being alone. With Daniel's return, I have a family again. I have made a lot of wonderful, and the most amazing one of them has just arranged for us to get together and talk whenever I want.

How did I come up with that verbal command phrase so quickly? I never got that dog I hoped for, but my new arrangement Angel has the potential to be even better. The command phrase came easily.

"Here, Spot. Good Boy!"

Granted that a glowing alien orb is not exactly just a "spot," but who would name their new best friend, "Orb?"]

Appendix Angel's report to the Vatican

Report: EYES ONLY – HIS HOLINESS

From: Fr. Gustaf Richter

[Formerly of the Vatican Office of Paranormal Events

Now Head of the Vatican Office of Extraterrestrial Affairs]

Topic: Brief Introductory Summary of Reports being complied by alien

"Guardian" AI, aka, Angel

Purpose: To provide a context for evaluating the much larger and more detailed set of reports that will follow.

[*Translation note, some of this material is extremely old and complied from multiple sources to form a coherent narrative. When the data is unclear, this report will include the multiple terminology rather than make an unverifiable random redaction*.]

Preface from the AI, Angel: Humanity's story begins with the ancient ones, the makers, the first minds. There are lots of names in the archives but no clear indication of how they referred to themselves. Maybe they were around when the earth's sun was settling down and the planet was forming or maybe it was a bit more recent. Surely, they were gone by at least 4 million years ago. So how do we even know about them? There were a few claims that some artifacts had survived from their time, but none have been verified. Their existence seems to be the most logical conclusion to the evidence that various species have been gathering for a very long time, and stories that are part of their racial memory. The most significant information comes from data programed into the very first orbs. Though the first orbs were improved, reprogrammed, and given new missions, they do retain some of their original knowledge. Each orb is capable of self-repair and self-replication but over countless millennia some data seems to have been 'overwritten" or garbled. Here is the most common version of the story they preserved:

Some form of life is common throughout the galaxy but most of it remains basic and rather uncomplicated because a very distinct set of conditions – referred to by humans as the "goldilocks zone" - are necessary for higher lifeforms to evolve and by random change those circumstances are inevitable when there are billions of solar systems in this galaxy alone – and here you can read divine intervention and purpose if you are so inclined.

A very long time ago, and for the first time anywhere in our galaxy, a lifeform achieved conscious self-awareness. Whatever form that was, it evolved into a technical and highly advanced civilization. Eventually, this civilization asked the question that always arises: "Are we alone?" They sent out a call, and time passed, and no one answered. They managed to develop a type of faster than light interstellar travel, but the method was deadly to living matter or, at least, it was deadly to them. So, they sent forth 'seekers' – current humans would identify those seekers as self-replicating AI. The seekers' purpose was to look for other intelligent life. A long period of time passed [data unclear] and the seekers reported back that they did indeed find life, an abundance of life, but none of it self-aware or highly evolved.

It is claimed the first ones never ventured beyond their own planet – or perhaps read "their own solar system" – because their method of interstellar travel did not accommodate their own biology. Setting aside their disappointment at finding a galaxy empty of fellow sentients, they boldly – or desperately - decided to embark on "the mission." The terminology used seems to indicate that the ancient ones were spiritually inclined and saw this "mission" as their divinely appointed task.

The original "seekers" were given new abilities and a new purpose [some sources refer to this second mission as "the uplift"]. In some texts this second wave is called "makers" or "designers." Now they were sent forth to evaluate the lifeforms they found and, if possible, try to modify their genetic code to encourage the rise of sentient beings. Most of the time conditions were not conducive to higher life but a few locations were, and the process pushed local evolution on to a new path. The number of sentient life forms throughout the galaxy is unknown; the lowest estimate is about 100 different species. There is no high estimate because achieving sentience is a slow process and there is not a clear marker as to when that goal is achieved.

[Data is unclear here] Maybe it is the way things normally should flow or maybe there was some flaw in the genetic tampering they used but those lifeforms evolved very, very slowly. What the ancient ones had achieved in less than 100 thousand years, it was estimated that their "children" would take several million years to reach. Even as the new lifeforms became more intelligent, change happened more by accident than by design. They seemed to be lacking the very characteristics that had set the ancient ones on their noble mission. Apparently lacking imagination, curiosity or ambition, the offshoot civilizations evolved at a steady but glacial pace. It is also possible that the slower progress was due to the fact that most of these beings have a much longer lifespan – as much as 500 years – than the average human. With so much time to use, there is little impetus to move quickly.

By the time this information came back to them, the ancient ones were truly ancient by now. It is unclear whether they had grown feeble, or their civilization was the end of its lifecycle, some speculate that frustrated by their loneliness, they were abandoning this more physical life to transcend to something higher/different/spiritual.

Before they vanished entirely from history, the last of them sent out a few emissaries with a slightly different mission. They were to spark new sentient life but be much more involved in its development. Where the previous mission was to light a spark and let in develop on its own, the new group were intended to instill their charges/children/experiments with something very close to the ancient ones' own genetic propensity for imagination and curiosity.

The AI sent out on this last mission were the most advanced and had the most independence. These "guardians" could not be programed as rigidly as the first two missions. They would have to adjust and so they were designed to self-correct and themselves evolve. Their only imperative was to guard these new creatures because these "children of the ancient ones" would be genetically programed to evolve quickly, to seek and to dare the uncharted.

The guardians first understood their mission was to provide as much assistance as the newly developing human civilization could absorb. Each time that ended in disaster and the few survivors would start over again. After several attempts resulted in "lost civilizations," the guardians refrained from overt involvement in human advance. Civilizations would still rise and fall but never with the cataclysmic destruction of the early failures. Compared to other alien species, the humans did advance rapidly, perhaps even at a pace comparable to the ancient ones.

In recent times [*data estimate at approximately 50,000 years*] other star traveling species did discover humanity, often called "the new ones." The other species had taken as much as 100 million years to achieve interstellar travel. When humans were first discovered, they seemed to be appropriately primitive for a race out on the edge of the galaxy – it would have taken even the seekers of the first mission a long time just to get here. But each time the others returned, humanity's speed of advance was startling.

The societies on other worlds are generally more uniform than the diversity and divisions found on earth. It is unclear if that is a genetic trait or simply the fact that they have been around so very long that they have had the time to resolve their differences. Most of these societies have a belief in a deity and traditions that might be termed spiritual or religious. A few are a bit more agnostic. It is significant to note that the grays, the most frequent visitors to earth, are among them.

The current visitors [of several species] think that earth might be the one instance where the ancient ones' last experiment succeeded. Some are in awe of humanity and the potential found there; some are afraid that you are advancing too fast and may burn yourselves out rather quickly; and, of course, some just fear humans because you move too fast, you aren't like them, and they fear that you could soon overwhelm them. They fear that humanity might literally be the ancient ones reborn on surrogate earth but unlike those ancient ones, you aren't alone, and they fear that you might not be happy with the company.

Suggested Action Items from Dr Richter:

- Ask Angel to specifically search for information on alien religions and spiritual beliefs.

- Prepare an encyclical, for later release, that will show a commonality of belief across the galaxy, in easy, layman's terms.

- Attempt to establish contact with those alien species that do not show hostility toward humanity.

- Slowly introduce the broad concepts of non-human religious experience into seminaries and universities.

- Pray that the aliens find nothing to fear from us.

- Thank God for our Guardian Angel

Made in the USA
Middletown, DE
09 October 2023